MW01253630

Prodigal Slave

Roxy Harte

ELLORA'S CAVE
ROMANTICA®
ELLORASCAVE.COM

An Ellora's Cave Publication

www.ellorascave.com

Prodigal Slave

ISBN 9781419971495
ALL RIGHTS RESERVED
Prodigal Slave Copyright © 2011 Roxy Harte
Edited by Jillian Bell.
Cover design by Syneca.
Cover photography by Brenda Carson/Shutterstock.com.

Electronic book publication December 2011
Trade paperback publication 2014

Chapter One

ဢ

The blood-red velvet bustier lying inside the half-open box on top of my bed was unexpected. It had arrived via Federal Express. Once I realize what it is, I don't dare lift it from its pristine nest of white tissue.

I open the card and read *Happy Birthday*. There is no signature, no identifying mark. "What the heck?"

I haven't celebrated my birthday in a very long time. Not since I turned thirty-five.

I'm certain my entire face frowns. I can't begin to imagine who would send me such an erotic, very expensive gift. Not my daughters, definitely not my ex-husband, John, and as for suitors or even potential suitors…don't make me laugh. The delivery was a mistake. It has to be a mistake, but oh, what a very, very nice mistake I think as I lift the heavily boned corset from the box. Dare I even look at the size?

No. I hold it up, not daring. It looks as if it will fit. Surely to god John wouldn't send me something so extravagant. I turn it so I can hold the cups over my boobs, smoothing the front over my midriff. Checking the mirror over my dresser, I think I look only slightly ridiculous holding the very sexy lingerie over my work clothes.

I think it will fit.

"Okay, it's a mistake," I tell my reflection. My reflection argues back, "It only coincidentally arrived on your birthday…in the correct size."

Since I'm two-thirds of the way to ancient, who knows if I will ever, ever have an opportunity to try on something so lavish again. My reflection looks back at me with a twinkle in her eyes. Oh no, I remember that look. "I am not twenty years old."

My reflection wiggles, dying to try it on.

"I'm too old. And too fat."

"I have no one to wear this for!"

I bounce in front of the mirror, finally unable to contain myself a moment longer. I know it's wrong, but I won't get it dirty. I'll just try it on for a little fun before breaking out the frozen dessert and pouting the rest of the night because I'm alone on my birthday. "Deal?" I ask my reflection and my mirror image nods willingly.

The devil himself couldn't make a more twisted bargain.

Peeling off my silk blouse and bra, I unhook the fifty-odd hooks lining the back of the corset, wondering how I will ever be able to put it on even for fun without help, and there is absolutely no one I would go to for help with this. In a moment of inspiration, I put it on backward, sucking in and hooking all of the lower hooks before twisting it back around to adjust my breasts in the cups. I turn to look in the mirror and sigh, "Wow," sounding a little shocked, feeling a whole lot awed. When was the last time I saw myself?

Sure, I see myself every day. Quick glance when I brush my hair and teeth, closer focus applying makeup, cellulite update when I climb into the shower...but to see myself like this. *Sexy*. Yeah, it's been awhile.

I lift the original Federal Express packaging to find out the name and address of the correct recipient, expecting it to be for Chianti, the tall, leggy blonde with blue eyes as big as saucers and a tan to die for who lives in the Cape Cod across the road that is a mirror twin of my own, but instead find the addressee to be Cassiopeia. "Fuck. Fuckfuckfuck!"

I twist fabric, unhook hooks and wrench the bustier off, feeling absolutely ridiculous. Tossing the lush scarlet velvet back into the box, I tuck it in, hide it beneath the tissue.

I think I threw the packaging across the room because I have to cross the room to retrieve it, knowing my vision is playing tricks on me. Alzheimer's perhaps? I am, after all, forty-five today. Or an acid trip flashback...though I've never experienced such an episode before... I suppose twenty-five years post-experimentation it could happen.

With a shaking hand, I pick the packaging off the ground and with eyes half-squinted peek again, reading through the blur. Cassiopeia. "Holy mother of god."

I sit quickly on the carpeted floor...to keep from falling down. "It can't be. It can't be. It can't be." And really, it couldn't be. No one has called me Cassiopeia in nineteen years and then, only He called me by my slave name. Master.

Those days are so long past, another lifetime, it seems unreal. I really was the girl he'd called Cassiopeia, not my real name, Charlotte, or the name the sorority girls lovingly called me, Charley, but my slave name. Had I really called him Master? Had I really been a sex slave?

God, it seems so incredible...so unlikely...I mean, it happened. I remember those days, have thought about those days in the dark of the night. Or at least I used to think about those days in the hours I couldn't sleep when I masturbated to John's soft snores, but I haven't thought about that lifetime, or Master...in almost twenty years. God, has it really been that long? Yes, I decide, because my twin girls are eighteen.

I'm suddenly glad they left for a European summer vacation with their grandparents two weeks ago. How would I ever explain this?

I start laughing when I see the itty-bitty piece of velvet on the floor that pretends to be some form of panty, though in my mind a triangle of velvet and strips of elastic do not a pair of panties make.

Once they did, a voice in my head reminds me. *Once you had an entire closet of such deliciously naughty things to wear. Remember?*

I take a deep breath, seeking my girls' smiling faces framed on the wall, confirmation that yes, I am a mother. I've spent eighteen years being Mommy, just Mommy, and I've been a great mommy. I went to parent-teacher conferences, PTO meetings, coached their soccer team. I made cookies—not just any cookies, but the best damn chocolate chip espresso cookies known to man, and I can rightfully proclaim so because I won a contest at the state fair three summers ago. I even have a plaque that reads Best Damn Cookies Known to Man—Illinois State Fair.

I am Mommy.

I am Charlotte Sullivan, paralegal extraordinaire.

I am not Cassiopeia.

Once, but not now. The gift was a mistake…or a joke…and if it was a joke it was a damn cruel joke.

Standing, I wipe my eyes, trying to forget who I once was, trying to forget what I once meant to the man I called Master. He cherished me. Bending to pick up the spent packaging with every intention of re-boxing the birthday gift and returning to sender, I have to wipe my eyes again, not believing this stupid joke is making me cry.

The memories flood back with my tears. He had loved me, he begged me not to leave, but he didn't love me enough to keep me. That was my argument. "If you love me as much as you say you do, you will give me a baby. I've never asked anything of you before. Never. I'm asking for this now."

He had refused and like a thief in the night, I disappeared and quickly, very quickly, found a man I deemed good enough to father my child. John Phillips. Remembering it all, I can't believe I'd pushed that year from my mind so easily. I'd cried myself senseless missing Master, but with my biological clock ticking, managed to see John through the blur. He'd been my art appreciation professor years before, and I'd bumped into him at a donut shop. We took the time to catch up on each other's lives and, over a glazed donut and coffee, I decided he would father my child, so I seduced him. It wasn't difficult…I was wearing a very revealing halter top at the time…and very, very short shorts. Ten months later, I had my twin girls.

In the time in between meeting and babies, I agreed to marry him, because it was the right thing to do even though I didn't love him. I promised myself I would learn to love him, but I never did. I grew quite fond of him, but I honestly never fell in love with him…and he never really fell in love with me either, though he protested he did. I didn't believe him, and the string of coeds in and out of his bed was proof enough he didn't love me. Divorce was easy once we decided we could, that it would be okay, it was the right thing to do. Taking back my maiden name was as easy as signing on a line marked with an X. If not for the twins, it would be as if the nineteen years between had never happened.

The ringing phone interrupts my thoughts.

"Hello?"

"Mommy!"

"Ellie?" My heart jumps in my chest, hearing my daughter's voice. I rush to the bed, pushing the opulent bustier deeper into the folds of delicate tissue. I know she can't see me, definitely can't see what's lying on my bed, but I need to hide it. Need to hide myself. Yanking on my shirt, skipping the bra, I ask, "Are you okay? Is anything wrong? My god, it's the middle of the day here…what time is it?"

"I dunno…late…I miss you."

"I miss you too, baby. Where's your sister? Sleeping? Is that your radio? Geez, Ellie, you're going to wake everyone in the hotel. Turn it down so I can hear you." I finish buttoning my blouse and slam the lid down over the tissue paper, fumbling a bit, wondering why things never go back into the box as easily as they come out. I settle for shoving the box under the bed, hands shaking so badly the lid pops off and I don't even try to fit it back on.

"You sound weird, Mom. Are you okay?"

"I'm fine. Just fine." I kick the box farther out of view. "The radio, Ellie, I can barely hear you."

"Oh, it's not the radio. We're at a disco. Can you believe they really have discothèques here? Amsterdam is so cool," Ellie gushes, and then I hear her say, "Oh hell" before the phone clatters, leaving me with all manner of awful flying through my brain.

"Ellie? Ellie! Answer me! You're at a club?"

"Mom?"

"Ellie?"

"Yeah, I'm here. Sorry, I dropped the phone when Bree upchucked all over her dance partner."

"Dance partner? Ellie? Where are your grandparents?" I do the quick math in my head, figuring if it is 4:00 p.m. here it is 1:00 a.m. there. "Get Bree away from that man. I want you back at the hotel right now!"

"Mom…Mom. It's cool. She didn't drink that much. Geez."

"Drinking? She's drinking? As in alcohol? What were you thinking letting your sister drink so much she's throwing up? She could have alcohol poisoning! She could be dying even as we speak. Are you drinking too? Ellie?"

"Mom. Stop. Bree is not going to die. She hardly drank anything at all. It's probably the brownies. I think she ate too many when she went to the café with Grandpa. Geez, she hasn't stopped eating since. Did you know kids start drinking here about twelve?"

"Kids do not start drinking at twelve. Maybe sixteen but not twelve and you, young lady, are American, not European, so rules still apply…no drinking." I realize I'm shouting and then a terrible thought hits me. "Your grandpa took Breeney to a café? What kind of café?"

"Aw, Mom, you know. Grandpa even told you he was going to check out the Mary J coffee shops when he hit Amsterdam."

"Tell me you did not smoke dope!" I shriek.

"No. And neither did Bree, she just ate brownies. Hell, I didn't even go. I went with Grandma. You never told me how much fun she is!"

I don't dare imagine.

"We went shopping."

Thank god. At least one child spent an untainted afternoon.

"We went to the Red Light District but don't freak out, we were safe 'cause it was like morning and did you know Amsterdam is rated like one of the safest cities in the world? So don't worry," Ellie explains fast, giggling. "Grandma bought a real French maid outfit. Not one of those cheap Halloween costume kinds but the real deal. Oh my god, Mom, you will never believe this thing. It's short. I mean really, really short, a black dress with white ruffles under the skirt and everything. She even got stockings and a garter belt…and oh my god, a feather duster."

The vision is clear in my mind. Oh god.

I listen to my daughter laughing hysterically on the other side of the world, wishing I were there, wishing I knew how much she'd already had to drink and wishing I could kill both of my parents. How dare they? These are my precious babies for crying out loud. I want to think homicidal thoughts but my brain keeps going to the image of my sixty-four-year-old mother dressed in a French maid outfit. I start to laugh hysterically, because the whole situation is too bizarre. Seeing the edge of the box peeking out from under the bed and knowing what I'm trying to hide, I laugh harder. And I was worried about them seeing that.

"Mom? Have you been drinking? You sound drunk."

Tears stream over my cheeks. I hear Ellie telling Bree to talk because the guy she's been waiting to dance with all night is waiting for her.

"Hi-ya, Mom-m-my. It's Bri-an-na."

"Hi, baby." I sober up hearing her sounding very drunk. I wipe my face on the long sleeve of my shirt. "You shouldn't drink any more, okay? I want you to promise me you won't and take your sister back to the hotel. Your grandparents are probably worried sick."

"Nah, they're cooool. You never told me what cool parents you have."

"I never realized myself." Oh hell, that's a lie. I distinctly remember being thirteen the first time I stole a toke from one of my parents' many long-haired, tie-dyed friends' joints. Our house was always crowded…musicians, artists, antiwar protesters…there was always plenty of beer, pot and space to crash. Dear god, whatever made me believe I should let my parents take my children out of the country? Whatever was I thinking? "Where are your grandparents?"

"They're here. They're upstairs in the hotel room."

"The discothèque is located in the hotel?"

"Well, duhhhhhh. You don't think Grandma and Grandpa would let us roam the streets of an unfamiliar town in a foreign country do you?" Her sarcasm is extra thick as she asks, "Reaaally, Mom?"

"Of course they wouldn't. What was I thinking?" I'm thinking I should catch the next plane to Amsterdam…that's what I'm thinking. "I'm coming to get you. This trip was a bad idea."

"Mom. No. We're fine. Besides, tomorrow is going to be like totally bor-ring. That's why we're having a little fun tonight because tomorrow the tour bus goes to like a zillion windmills and a friggin' tulip farm. Ooh-ee, that'll be some real excitement. Besides, we're being good. Grandpa said no absinthe and we haven't drunk any because he said if we did you'd never forgive him and he didn't want you to be mad, okay? So we're being good. Don't be mad. Look, I gotta go. This is the last dance before they close for the night. I love you. I'll call you tomorrow."

"Bree? Bree. Call me tonight. Call me as soon as you are in the hotel room and safe."

A dial tone is my answer. Well, hell. Thanks, Dad. Way to make them be good. Pot-loaded brownies are okay but hallucinogenic beverages are not. Holy mother of god, what was I thinking, trusting my babies to the care of my parents?

Sitting down on my bed, I force myself to stay sitting and not race to the airport as if I were a lunatic. "They're fine," I tell myself. "They're with my parents." Funny, that doesn't make me feel as confident as it should. The phone rings in my hand and I jump, "Breeney?"

"No," a man says with a slight accent. "Try again?"

Frankie? Gorgeous, incredible, charismatic, once-upon-a-time-I-would-have-died-for-one-more-mind-bending-fuck Frankie? Hell, Frankie, as in the other lifetime Frankie better known as Master, Frankie?

More precisely the Master I'd deserted in order to marry the Professor.

"Cassiopeia?"

"Please don't call me that, Frankie. That was a long time ago."

"Time hasn't changed the way I feel about you."

I am stunned into silence. Is this a cruel joke? After almost twenty years, he decides it is time to get even with me for leaving him? Is he that sadistic? I don't answer. Once I was bound to this man...heart, mind, body and soul. Bound more tightly by emotion and need than I could ever have been bound by any physical means...rope, steel, leather...and so it was only greater emotion and need that could tear us apart. My biological clock. I can feel the emotion behind the tick-tock, tick-tock as if it was only yesterday.

He announces, "I saw Paulette."

Ah, Paulette. That explains everything. Mutual friend from the old days, big-mouthed gossip then, bigger-mouthed gossip now…and running with the same crowd. "So how is Paulette?"

"You should know. You had lunch with her last week."

Ouch, terse. Swallowing, I decide silence is the best way to handle this very strange flash from my past life.

"You and John divorced?"

"Yes," I whisper, wondering if this conversation could get any stranger. Hell, could this day get any weirder? John. I rarely even think about him. Sad, since I once really liked him. He'd guaranteed an intelligent gene pool for making babies and over our almost two decades of marriage we'd shared two-point-five kids (two of our own and one of his from a previous marriage who stayed with us summers), a dog and a vacation home on the lake. We never grew beyond liking each other though.

"Paulette showed me pictures of Briana and Elizabeth."

I close my eyes, imagining Frankie holding the wallet-sized pictures of my daughters.

"They're beautiful. They look so much like you." He sighs over the phone.

I laugh. Yes, they do resemble me a lot…when I was younger…much younger. "They look a lot like I did. You're right about that." I wonder what else Paulette shared.

"Are they having a good time in Europe?"

Ah hell, Paulette. Is nothing sacred between friends anymore?

"Too much fun by my barometer."

"Yes, Paulette said you'd changed."

What?

"So you're single for the summer. Any wild, crazy plans for you?"

Snorting, I wonder where on earth this more-peculiar-by-the-second phone conversation is leading. At forty-five I find my wild single life is defined by what brand of ice cream is on sale. Like my plans for this evening for example—wild, as in a quart of double-brownie death-by-decadence triple-fudge ice cream, and single, as in sharing said decadence with Jay Leno at midnight. "What do you want, Frankie?"

"Did you open my gift yet?"

"Yes. I can't imagine what you were thinking." I catch my reflection in the mirror and, tucking a stray curl, look a little harder...sucking in, standing taller. I suck in more, holding my breath.

"I was thinking it's your birthday. You are divorced. And you are still mine. I want you home. Now."

The breath I'd been holding comes out in a forced rush, my stomach popping back out the two inches I'd almost hidden.

"Come to me, Cassiopeia," Frankie commands and it is as days of old. The memories return in a crazed rush—me kneeling at his feet, wearing his collar...me, pulling a pony cart at the Slave Games. *Holy mother, that wasn't me.* Really. It's my memory but it couldn't have been me. I inhale, exhale, dots forming behind my eyes, phone shaking uncontrollably in my hand.

"Now. Cassiopeia. Come to me, now."

Beep. Beep.

It's a full second before I realize my call waiting is desperately trying to gain my attention. "Frankie, I couldn't. It's been nineteen years." *Beep. Beep.*

"Can you hold a minute, please? I have to take this...it's my daughter...one of my daughters."

"Go, go," he insists. "I'll wait." *I've been waiting twenty years, what's another moment?* My mind says the unsaid as I switch over to the other line.

"Hello?"

"Hi-ya, Mommy. It's Breeeeeee. We're back in the hotel room all safe and sound, so you can stop worrying now."

I hear Ells in the background, "Safe and sound. Love you."

"Just ignore Ellie. She's way too hap-py. She thinks she's in lo-ove."

"What?" I exclaim, really ready to get on the next flight to Amsterdam.

"Don't worry, Grandpa wouldn't let him come in the room. Besides, he's an art history major minoring in education. What a loser. It'll never last, so no worries."

Art history major? Education? Oh hell, she's falling for a young version of her father? What was I thinking, letting them go off to Europe without me? "Tell her no dating while she's on foreign soil."

"Grandpa already told her that."

"Let me talk to your grandfather."

"Can't. He went to bed with Grandma." Bree giggles. "Did Ellie tell you about the French maid costume? Oh my god. It was hil-ar-i-ous on the hanger...you should see it on Grandma."

I hear Ells hiss in the background, "Let me talk."

"Wait, Ellie. Gosh," Bree tells her sister, then to me says, "I'm gonna go to bed now. I love you."

I smile. "I love you too, baby. Good night."

"It's me," Ells tells me, having taken over the phone and relays to her sister, "Mom said she loves you," before coming back to me. "Mom? Bree says she loves you too, and I love you. I miss you."

"I miss you too." Tears fill my eyes and I wipe them hastily away.

"We are officially safe and sound in our hotel room. So stop worrying."

"Okay, I'll try."

"No. Promise," she insists. "I want you to have fun this summer. Get out and meet some people. Meet a man. You deserve to be happy again."

I smile, my face screwing up as I try not to cry, thinking how grown-up she actually sounds over the phone.

"I am happy," I insist.

"Yeah, yeah," she mocks. "Don't be mad at us about today, okay? We were just blowing off a little steam. You know we're good kids, right?"

I assure her, "Yes, baby, I know you're good kids."

"Okay. Just so you know. I love you."

"I love you too." I wipe more tears away, trying not to sob out loud because my chest is aching so much with missing them. "I'll talk to you tomorrow."

"Yep. Just like we promised. You will hear our happy, safe and sound voices every day. So you won't have to worry."

"I'll worry anyway," I promise.

"'Kay, Mommy. Good night."

Click.

"Good night, baby."

"It's me."

Oh hell, I think to myself, hearing Frankie's voice. Shaking my head, I try to wake myself up from the dream I'm having. It's too surreal hearing my daughters' voices from so far away seeming so much as if they are in the next room, and then Frankie's voice filling my brain in the very next sentence. I gasp, "Frankie."

"Come to me."

I shake my head, finally finding my voice to say, "That isn't possible."

It's been too long. I'm not the same woman, even if you are still the same man.

But two decades hasn't been enough time to forget the thrill in the pit of my stomach every time I've caught a whiff of leather over the years, not enough time to quell the instant wetness that coated the inside of my thighs the second I heard the timbre of his commanding voice, and definitely not long enough to still the pounding of my heart as it tries to leap through my ribs at the mere thought of being held in his arms once more, post-flogging. What am I thinking? That I can just rush off to meet him as in the good old days? The key word here being old…as in I am old, used up, done. Not to mention twenty pounds heavier if the mirror and my jeans size are to be believed.

"Anything is possible, Cassiopeia, if you are willing."

"Please, Frankie, I haven't been called Cassiopeia in a very long time. We were kids then, playing a kids' game. You can't really expect me to meet you just like that, can you? I have responsibilities."

"It was never a game, Charlotte. I'm sorry you thought it was."

Click.

The dial tone buzzes in my head several seconds before I realize he hung up on me. And he called me Charlotte. Frankie has never, ever called me Charlotte. *Damn. Damn. Damn.*

Chapter Two

❧

The bustier fits, as in fits like a glove. It seems custom-made just for me. I don't know why I had to try it on again. Maybe because it's my birthday, and I can't stop thinking about the birthdays I shared with Him. Or maybe because sitting on my bed eating spoonfuls of ice cream I couldn't concentrate on Jay Leno's jokes because I kept smelling His aftershave. And a quick peek under the bed revealed that yes, he'd sprinkled his aftershave on the tissue paper.

So just to prove to myself the impossibility of going to him, I bravely pulled the sinfully soft, heavily boned garment from its packaging...to prove to myself I am not that girl anymore. But then I buried my nose in his scent...and then I was naked, sliding into the velvet bustier and matching thong. Big mistake. I wasn't expecting to think I looked good — ridiculous maybe, but not enticing...

Yet, standing in front of the full-length closet mirror, I *see* myself. Maybe for the first time in two decades. I am a very erotic creature.

I've still got it!

Yes, I'm forty-five, but with the bustier, my figure is almost as good as when I was twenty-five...unbelievable but true. Yes, I've filled out a bit, curvier but luscious now in a way I never was then. I touch my pushed-up breasts, appreciating the way the soft fabric feels against my skin. The memory of who I once was, what I once was tumbles from the dark closet in my brain that has held those thoughts checked for so long.

I was the sex slave of Master François Rene de Hart.

I was loved, beloved, cherished. Collared. Owned.

Lying across my bed, I close my eyes, remembering a night Master was in a playful mood.

"Touch yourself."

Without any self-consciousness, I did, sliding my fingers through my wet folds. I'd lingered over my clit, rubbing, teasing. He'd watched…every tantalizing swirl of my fingers, back and forth…he'd watched and he'd encouraged me, "Taste yourself."

Without missing a stroke, I'd lowered my left hand to dip a finger inside my wet pussy while the fingers of my right hand kept up their erotic dance over my ultrasensitive clit. With thick cream evident on my fingertips, I'd lifted them to my mouth, sticking my tongue out to lick and swirl, tasting before pushing my fingers deep into my mouth to suck.

Without embarrassment, I'd touched myself, tasted myself and had the orgasm of my life while he watched.

Was I too hasty in denying him tonight?

Smoothing my hand over my midriff, I feel the softness of the velvet, the sharpness of the boning. I slide my hand lower to touch myself, feeling my own slickness and, for a brief second, it feels incredible, but then I realize what I'm doing and I feel absolutely ridiculous. What am I thinking? After almost twenty years, the girl he called Cassiopeia is a stranger to me. He too is a stranger. I have no idea where he's been, what he's been doing or who he's been doing it with.

I tell my girls all the time, "You have to be careful. It's a dangerous world. In my day sex couldn't kill you — now it can. Get to know the boys you date and don't rush into anything. Find out their history."

Yes, they roll their eyes and make jokes. "Could you please fill out your complete history of sexual partners and note when and if you ever contracted any sexual diseases? Yeah, Mom, that'll go over real well. You must really want us to stay virgins the rest of our lives."

I don't. I just want them safe. I don't want them to fall into promiscuity as I did in college. I close my eyes, knowing Frankie had saved me from myself by convincing me to be his slave. I suddenly wish I hadn't been so eager to dismiss him, though not for sex, not for Master/slave games, but to catch up. We could have met for coffee and chatted about our lives since the last time we saw each other, and maybe our sexual histories would have come up. Just in case we decided we might want to revisit the past...just a little.

I know my side would have been a very limited addition to the conversation. "Let's see, there was John Phillips, no STDs, not even so much as a cold sore."

Rather remarkable really, considering John's promiscuity with the coeds.

It suddenly occurs to me that what I've been preaching to my daughters applies to me. Technically, by having sex with John, knowing he was having sex with others, I'd slept with all of his partners...I could have a sexually transmitted disease and not even know it. Ewww.

I pick up the phone and call John.

"Hello?" He sounds sleepy.

I look at the bedside alarm clock. One a.m. Yes, he's been asleep for hours. Well, too bad, this is important. "Did you catch any STDs while we were still married?"

"What? Who is this? Charlotte, is that you?"

"Yes, John, I know there are a hundred other woman who might potentially call you at one a.m. No, let me revise, I know there are a lot of *girls* out there who might—"

"Hey, I take offense to that."

"You shouldn't, the truth is the truth. You've slept with a lot of young girls—"

"They've all been of age."

"And I want to know if any of them ever gave you an STD while we were married?"

21

"You called me at one o'clock in the morning to talk about STDs?"

"Answer the question, John."

"Why do you want to know?" he asks suspiciously.

"Oh my god," I say, "You did! What did you bring home, John? Gonorrhea, Syphilis?" I jump out of bed, pacing, feeling dirty even though we've been divorced a year and stopped having sex three or four years before that. Dirtier because now I am thinking about this the way I should have been thinking about it all along…

"God, no, Charlotte. I never brought anything home. Why are you asking now? Are you sick? Is there something wrong?"

For a moment the concern I hear in his voice is a comfort. Once we were very comfortable together. Once we were friends enough that even though we didn't love each other the way a husband and wife should, we could at least comfort each other. "No, John. I'm fine. I only wanted to know because I might start dating again and I needed to know I was safe."

The silence coming from the other end of the phone is deafening, followed by a very terse, "You know they have STD testing now. You could have gone to the University clinic for free and had every test known to man run and I could still be sleeping."

"I wanted to hear it from your mouth first, John." I match his harsh tone, realizing we can't even be friends anymore. "I'll still have the tests done, but I wanted to hear you say I wouldn't need to worry about the results."

Hanging up, I breathe a huge sigh of relief. We might not be friends anymore, but I still trust him, even though I have absolutely no reason to believe a single word he says. I resolve to call the clinic first thing in the morning, even though the Pap smear I had done three months ago was fine.

I scroll through my received call list, my thumb poised to redial the only number I don't recognize. I press, it dials, Frankie answers. "*Oui?*"

His French accent stirs something deep within my core...memory, desire, need. It was always so. Just hearing his voice fuels my lust for him.

"I want to know your sexual history, I want a clean bill of health stating you are STD-free, and I want to catch up over coffee. My god, Frankie, you call after almost two decades and just expect me to pour myself into a velvet bustier and march over to your house?"

He laughs and then he says, "*Oui, j'attends cela.*"

He expects that? "Well, you can just get over yourself. It's a different world than it was twenty years ago."

He sighs. "Tomorrow is Saturday. Meet me at Brahm's."

* * * * *

As I open the door, a small bell tinkles and I am transported back in time. I inhale the scent of freshly baked pastries and fresh brewed German coffee. Brahm's Café hasn't changed in twenty years—not the wallpaper, not the artwork, not the tables and chairs. As I cross the room to meet Frankie, it seems nothing has changed at all. From a dozen paces I feel the connection between us sizzle and I am drawn to him.

I stop walking though I am still paces away from him, fighting uselessly against his tug as I realize I am still his...heart, mind, body...and if I didn't know better, soul, because it seems whatever chemistry we once shared hasn't diminished at all. He is still gorgeous, his eyes sparkle as brightly blue as they ever did before and their allure is unmarred by the fine lines that appear when he smiles at me. His long, dark hair is still held in a ponytail at the nape of his neck, though the dark-brown hair is noticeably peppered with gray.

His dark-brown eyes are solemn as he stands and pulls out a chair.

I sit.

We are so formal with each other. We were always so formal. I never had with Frankie the relaxed mornings at the breakfast table sharing sections of newspaper as John and I did. Our mornings were structured. I knelt at his feet until I was bidden to do a task. I never wore clothing in the house, only my collar.

I try to imagine going home with Frankie…to stay…calling the house we once shared home. And then my daughters vault into the mental picture, bouncing and laughing…and I am at Frankie's feet. Naked. God. No. I can't do this to them.

I gasp and turn to flee, not taking the offered chair.

His hand on my shoulder stops me. I don't turn to look at him. "I can't do this. I had thought…"

"Thought what? That you missed me just a little? Enough to bring you here? Were you merely curious? Or did you dare to dream as I did?"

"I have children now."

"*Oui.*"

"I can't just parade about your house naked all day, wearing a collar."

"Why?" He shrugs as only a Frenchman can…suave, debonair, slightly arrogant. He challenges, "You enjoyed the lifestyle very much — once."

"I'm a grown woman, I have responsibilities."

He turns me to face him. His gaze catches mine and I melt under his — the lust, the love, the power is all still there in a single look. I am owned.

"It may be different than before out of necessity, but if you will return to me, anything can be possible."

"Do you believe that?"

"Yes, Charlotte. I believe if you will only let yourself, you will be Cassiopeia again." He lifts his eyebrow and nods toward the chair he pulled out. "I already ordered coffee and those small cakes you liked."

Glancing at the table, I bite my lip at the nostalgia. A part of me feels as though we dined here just yesterday.

"Stay and tell me about your daughters, if nothing else."

I take the seat, to be polite...and perhaps I am a bit curious about the last two decades he's spent without me. We sip hot coffee and eat sweet pastries. I tell him about my daughters and my career. I show him photographs of the twins. He reveals he moved back to his family's château in Saint-Émilion for a time after I left and stuns me when he takes my hand, admitting, "I couldn't stand being so far away from you, not knowing if you were safe and well. If you were loved. Cherished?"

My lips part and I try not to gape. How does one respond to that? I swallow hard, making sure my mouth is not open with a hard press of my lips together.

"I moved back to wait for the right time, so I might reclaim you."

"Oh." My fingertips fly to my face, covering my mouth. He reaches for my hand and pulls my fingers away, tugging slightly at my lower lip with his thumb as he does so. His touch electrifies me. I want to grab his hand, kiss his fingers, roll my tongue around his thumb but I sit there, no longer Cassiopeia. I am Charlotte Sullivan and paralegals do not lick men's fingers in public.

I bite my lower lip before taking another sip of coffee.

I want to kiss him the way I once kissed him...all teeth and tongue and raw passion. Oh god. I'm panting. I make excuses in my head. I want him so desperately because I haven't had sex...that's all. Really. It could be any man. It isn't any man. It's Frankie. Master.

Soccer moms do not pant with lust in public.

He asks me, "Remember when I told you I wanted to grow old surrounded by the vineyards and you at my side?"

I smile, remembering. I was so young and romantic then. I spent hours looking through books containing pictures of the French countryside and imagining moving there to be with my Frenchman François.

"After I returned, I would wake up there and want to share each simple moment with you. Early one morning I walked amid the vines while the dew was still glistening on the grapes and I thought, Cassiopeia should be here to see this with me."

My smile slips as I realize my heart aches with the memory of the lost dream. Fighting back tears, I wonder what is wrong with me. I look away, clearing my throat and trying to regain my composure. Damn him for sending that package. I blow out a soft breath, sure of my composure before I look back at him.

"Your daughters will go to France while they are in Europe?" he asks.

"Their first stop was London and I think their second was Paris," I answer with a smile. "They were in Amsterdam yesterday."

"And tomorrow?"

"Who knows?" I laugh, shrugging. "My parents…" I sigh and look away, thinking before I seek his gaze again. "I wouldn't know how to describe my parents. Hippies turned Republican as so many of their counterparts? Wandering souls who never look at a map but flutter like the golden leaves of autumn, falling wherever the wind takes them? Your guess is as good as mine as to where my children will be tomorrow."

"That makes you crazy."

"Yes, my parents make me crazy."

He smiles. "And yet you allowed them to go."

It is my turn to smile and laugh. "I survived my parents, and this is a trip they've been planning since the girls were in kindergarten. I couldn't disappoint them."

"You disappointed me," he reminds me, and the comment makes me uncomfortable. I bite my tongue, fighting the urge to say I am sorry because to do so would imply my regret in leaving him and I don't regret that, because if I'd never left, I wouldn't have my daughters. He surprises me by adding, "I don't blame you. Your family is beautiful."

"Thank you."

He looks at me and I fight to look away and lose — caught and held by his gaze. "You are mine."

Am I?

I tremble beneath his scrutiny and my eyes fill with tears. Because I am? Because I don't know that I am? Because I fear that I'm not?

"There is something you need to know," he says. "Something I never once told you, and I regret I never did."

I look at him expectantly, my heart kicking hard and fast against the wall of my chest. He takes my hand across the table, lifting my fingers to his lips, and with a single brush of his lips against my knuckles makes me feel what I have missed feeling for twenty years. I am the only woman in the world who matters to him.

"I love you, Cassiopeia. I have loved you from the moment we first met, and I will love you until the end of time."

Tears fall over my cheeks and I sob out the heartbreaking need I have longed to cry since the moment I opened the box. No. Since the moment I first walked out his door. He takes my hands and holds them to keep me from trying to hide my face, my tears, and demands, "Say it."

I choke through my tears, "I can't, not yet." I pant, hating this show of emotion. "It's been too long."

He reminds me, "You just said yet."

27

Chapter Three

ಬಿ

He waits for me. He had insisted I take the train instead of driving even though driving would have taken less than an hour. It was to be a journey separating myself from all that I was in the moments before I checked my baggage and stepped onto the train.

I'm a wreck. I chew a fingernail nervously, knowing as the train stops that this is it. There's no turning back now. I close my eyes. Thinking? Praying? Remembering? I wonder what in the hell I was thinking to board this train.

He stands at baggage waiting for me and as I cross to him I don't give a second thought to the fact that God, security and dozens of passengers are watching as I fall to my knees in front of him, tears streaming over my cheeks, my forehead bowed against his thighs. His hand wraps in my hair, pulling me to my feet, his lips gracing my forehead, whispering the words I've dreamed for two decades, "You have pleased me greatly this night, Cassiopeia."

In the car his hand caresses my knee as he drives me to his home, the home we'd once shared. My gut clenches as I remember the fully equipped dungeon hidden away in his basement. As if reading my mind his hand slides higher, cupping my tingling pussy, sending shivers and more up my spine. "Glad to be going home, love?"

"Home is in Glenview," I answer softly.

"No." His firm tone implies anger, though the look he gives me is soft, regret-filled. "Home was never there—with him—you belong to me. You always have and always will. Do you forget you wear my mark?"

My thoughts fly to a night twenty years ago when he branded my right ass cheek with his mark—a filigree heart. Heat flares there as it always does when I consider it. Once, I belonged to François Rene de Hart.

"No, I've never forgotten." I whisper, afraid of my own voice, adding even more softly, "Master."

His smile tells me he is pleased with my answer and he pats my knee before reaching up to untie the belt cinching closed my camel trench coat. Parting the cloth, he reveals scant velvet and indecent swells of flesh. Damn those twenty pounds and then some…more likely thirty by the figure revealed in the mirror before I'd fled my bedroom.

Self-conscious, I scan the dark horizon beyond the car window, pulling my lip between my teeth in an effort to hold back my tears.

"Look at me, Cassiopeia."

Hesitantly, I meet his eyes.

"First, welcome home."

My mouth makes an "O" as I realize we are going through the imposing iron gates.

"Second, you are no longer the young girl I lost. You have grown into an incredibly beautiful woman. And third—"

His pause brings my gaze back around to his as he parks in the garage, the door automatically lowering behind us. Gentle fingers trace my jawline and pull me forward into him for a painfully gentle, excruciatingly long, well-practiced kiss. When he finally releases my lips, I barely manage to croak, "Third?"

"You will now be punished for running away."

His answer is as short and abrupt as his exit from the car. Before I realize what he said, he is beside my door, opening it and helping me out, placing a firm hand on my elbow in case I harbor plans for escape.

Oh, hell. My mind races, my palms and armpits suddenly leaking buckets. Nervous chatter fills the air — me rambling. Arguments. "I don't deserve this. I came running when you summoned me, didn't I?" and "This was your fault. You knew my biological clock was ticking," and the true moment of desperation, "Everyone has to grow up sooner or later. It was time for me to grow up and give up silly games."

The last stopped him cold. We'd made it all the way to the final basement stair. He demands coldly, "Silly games?"

I stumble back a step.

His face, hidden in shadow, seems suddenly even more sinister with age than I'd remembered. It is the look he had once used to instill instant fear, but I am a mature woman now, intent on standing firm. It is all a game and to pretend otherwise is insanity. Twenty years has made me too old for games. I should have stayed in Glenview. But then, here I am, toe-to-toe and eye to eye with the man who'd filled the starring role in every fantasy I'd invented over those same years. Frankie. My Frankie. My Master. The one man in my life who'd never harmed me — not mentally, physically or emotionally.

So why am I suddenly shaking in my four-inch heels? It was never a game. It was our life together.

My mind flies back to the first time he led me down this same staircase.

"I'm afraid," I whisper — same words, same trembling voice as then. "I don't want any pain."

Master's face softens and I know he is remembering also.

"I promise I won't do anything you don't want me to do — anything you don't need me to do."

It is an echo, almost word for word, of the promise he'd made the night he'd introduced me to His World. His very real world. To him it was never a game at all. Suddenly, a lump fills my throat and tears are again streaming down my face. I fall to my knees for a second time in less than an hour, this time clutching his hand, pulling it to my lips. I kiss his fingers over and over again, sobbing, blubbering apologies, smearing tears and snot and spit over his knuckles until I can barely breathe.

Kneeling beside me, he pulls me into his arms.

"God, I've missed you, Cassiopeia."

I nod, not chancing words. In a heart-pounding, brain-spinning, sub-space-madness moment, I know I will agree to anything.

"I have to punish you. You know that, don't you? You understand you need me to punish you?"

I nod, burying my tear-streaked, snot-covered face into his shoulder. The twenty-year-veteran wife worries for an instant the mascara stain will be hell to get out of his tailored linen shirt. Then I beg, again in sub-space, promising to be good — if only — if only he won't cane me.

In that instant, he knows and I know…Cassiopeia is back. Begging, pleading, bratty Cassiopeia.

"Ask me to punish you, Cassiopeia."

I bury my head deeper, shaking it for all it is worth against the fabric of his shirt. Fabric saturated with his scent. I inhale deeply, savoring the moment, a brain tease for me.

Unfooled, he pushes me back, claiming my eyes. "Ask, Cassiopeia."

I tighten my jaw, shaking my head. Oh god, it is going to be so much worse on me now. *Oh goody. It is going to be so much worse.*

Master doesn't miss a beat, slapping my arrogant little face, not hard enough to bruise, just enough to get my full, undivided attention. Then his hands slide down my bare shoulders to the cups of the bustier. Rending fabric signals it was not only the first but also the last time it will ever be worn. An equally hard pull on the matching thong sees it torn off and flung to the ground.

31

Naked, I stand before him, a little less arrogant but still stubborn.

"Go home, Charlotte. I'm sorry I've wasted both our time tonight."

What? Whoa. This wasn't the way the game was played before. My foot stomps at his retreating shoulders as he takes the stairs two at a time.

He isn't coming back.

New choices, retreat and go home, or face Frankie and admit he's right, it isn't a game. It's his way of life or no way — at least not for us — and if I face the truth, the reason I ran in the first place, so many years ago, it was because his way of life was quickly becoming my way of life too, I got scared. Scared I might never be a normal person again.

And twenty years later, just as scared, just as sure his real life can never be my real life, our real life, because normal is what people are supposed to be. And deviant isn't part of normal. My life flashes before my eyes, a series of snapshots, the birth of my babies, a night of shed tears when I discovered the first of the coeds, more tears as I faced the loss of my sensuality, soccer games, PTA meetings, lonely nights lying next to a man I could barely still call friend let alone husband. I close my eyes, admitting to myself, "I am so done with normal."

I sigh, opening my eyes, looking at the door handle to the dungeon. I let my face fall into the door. "I don't know how to do this anymore." Hell, how does a mother of two face being a sexual deviant?

My hand closes over the door latch of the dungeon. It clicks open and I am standing inside before I realize I am "in" and not only in but breaking cardinal rule number one, never enter the dungeon without Master. Candles blaze from their wrought iron holders, hundreds of candles. Wax, leather, old sweat...the scent of my dreams...and my nightmares, waking to find I really am very far from home. My feet carry me to the display rack of floggers, horsewhips and rattan canes. Some I remember but most are unfamiliar toys. The irritated thought that Master has managed to keep busy over the years creeps through my brain...

Knees shaking, I reach for a cane I recognize, notched at one end for each time it had been used on me for true crimes. Twice, once for embarrassing him in front of other Doms at a New Year's Eve party, and once for not willingly using a second-tier safe word when I should have and ending up slightly injured by accident because of it.

There were three tiers of safe words. The first meant I was near the edge of all I could tolerate. It wouldn't stop play but it would slow play. The second meant I believed I was injured. Again it wouldn't stop play, but would alert Master to a problem he could address. Such would have been my case. I was hypothermic. God only knew if I would have safe-worded had I realized. I hadn't even realized. The third-tier word stopped all play immediately and would mean I no longer trusted Master's judgment to respond appropriately to a first- or second-tier word. It would mean immediate expulsion from the house since trust was all that held the bond together.

I remember my words as well as I remember my own name, Scooby-Doo, Cosmonaut and Peanut Butter and Jelly.

I slap the top of my thigh with the cane. A whoosh of dizziness finds me grabbing to hold on to the wall as the intelligent thought, "God, this baby hurts," parades through my brain.

"What are you doing, Charlotte?"

His voice echoes behind me and I know he still stands in the stairwell. Reaching beyond the toy rack, I retrieve a wicked-looking blade from a black-satin-covered table. Stage prop, but it serves its purpose as I hack notch number three into the cane.

"Charlotte?"

Less echo, threshold maybe.

Eyes adjusting, I force myself to search the dancing shadows for what I know is in the room. Somewhere. It has to be here. The only problem being my collar isn't in plain sight.

"Come, Charlotte. I'll drive you home."

"No." I turn to face him then, seeing what I hadn't noticed before, the barest edge of my collar, peeking out of his slacks pocket.

"My name is Cassiopeia. I belong to Master François Rene de Hart. See? I wear his mark upon my hip." I pivot and wiggle one hip, hoping I sound as seductive as I know I did so long ago. Turning back around, I catch his appreciative glance before he shutters away any emotion that might have peeked through. Stalking toward him, I state the facts. "I have been a very bad, bad girl. And now it is time to face my punishment, not as a bratty child who has to be forced, but as a grown woman who knows what she wants…and what she needs."

I am close enough to touch his cheek and do so with the edge of the cane, lifting his chin with the notched end. "The problem is, I am not sure my Master can handle a grown woman. The last time I saw him I was still a girl, easily managed, easily led."

His grinding jaw does little to hide the glint of humor escaping his eyes.

"I need to be punished, Master." Okay, I admit that was said way too sarcastically. I can't help myself.

"I am your Master, *oui*?"

Oh yeah. Definitely hit my mark.

"Yes. You are my Master."

His fingers snake into my hair and he pulls me into a painful kiss, reclaiming what was his, raping my mouth with his teeth and tongue. My scalp screams under the pressure. I taste blood. A second later I feel leather cinching around my throat. Blessed leather. My collar.

I am yours, Master, I am yours.

"On your knees, Cassiopeia, hands in front, forehead down."

Yeah, yeah, I know the drill. God, this is going to hurt.

"Lift your ass, bitch. It hasn't been that long. Do I have to re-teach you everything?"

The first strike draws a wide welt, just as I knew it would. I can't see it but pain shoots through my flesh, nerve endings screaming from tit to clit and I know it will leave a mark. My knees shake.

"Have you missed me, Cassiopeia?"

"Yes, Master."

I want him inside, reclaiming all of me, but it will take nineteen more strikes, one for each year I've been away before he stops. He runs his finger along the welt he made. "This is going to leave a beautiful mark, Cassiopeia."

"Yes-s," I hiss.

"You used to like it very much when I marked you," he comments.

"Yes-s." The anticipation of the next strike is killing me. I feel myself growing wet with need and he is toying with that need.

He taps my ass and thighs lightly with the cane. None were as devastating as the first. These are shadowy taps meant to keep me on edge, waiting for the next hard one. "Oh god," I moan. "I can't take this."

"But you will take this and more for me, won't you, Cassiopeia?"

I wiggle my ass, wanting the punishment to be completed. Nineteen welts for me to count, nineteen more welts that will turn to dark purple bruises. And over the next week, every time I sit, it will be with some discomfort...discomfort that will remind me I am his.

I imagine myself going to work on Monday, pulling my pantyhose over these marks, hiding them beneath a knee-length skirt and sitting behind my desk. No one else will know, but as I cross and uncross my legs, as I fidget in my seat, trying to get comfortable, I will be thinking of Master and grow wetter and wetter with need.

The cane swats against my thigh, making me jump and squeak with both surprise and pain. He admonishes me, "Pay attention, Cassiopeia. This is punishment for leaving, *oui*?"

"Yes-s."

"Yet you are enjoying it too much, I think."

"No," I lie.

Another swat falls and another. A third in rapid succession, making me gasp. "The truth now?"

"Yes, Master, I am enjoying it too much."

Four more lightning-quick swats make me jerk, my ass cheeks clenching tight. I swear, "Fuck," making him laugh. He asks, "Now it is starting to feel like punishment?" The cane falls four more times before I can answer. He asks, "How many has that been, Cassiopeia?"

"Thirteen," I say through gritted teeth.

He rubs his hand over my ass and thighs. "This is so very nice. Do you feel the welts when I rub my hand over them?"

"Yes-s."

"Beautiful marks," he sighs. "You always marked so wonderfully. Shades of blue are already peeking through the pink."

I wish I could see them.

"Do you remember how you used to stand in front of the mirror for hours, looking at the marks I'd leave on you?"

"I enjoyed having your mark on my body."

"*Oui*." He taps the cane gently against the welts, making my legs quiver. He strikes, making me gasp and jerk. He says, "That one was hard." He strikes again. Again. Again. Again. Again. That felt like the punishment he intended. He kneels beside me, turning my face to look into his. "You will not leave me again."

I am panting...pain, need, desire, doubt...all of it mixed up and rolled into one nameless emotion. My ass and thighs are on fire as his hands smooth over them. I want to promise him I will stay, that I will not leave, but I have others to think about. This isn't just about me. I can't allow myself to be the selfish hedonist I was before.

"How can we ever make this work?" I beg, wanting him to make me believe we can. "I'm a paralegal. I'm a mother."

"Do you want to make this work?"

I nod, closing my eyes because I want it so badly my raw need brings the sob from my chest the caning did not. His lips close over mine, promising me without words.

He stands, leaving me kneeling on my hands and knees. I watch him undress. He is older, we both are, and his age is reflected in a softening in his limbs, the black hair covering his chest is now peppered with gray, a slight paunch to his middle... But to my eyes, he is even more handsome, more sexy than he ever was in his prime. I watch him open a condom foil, then unroll the protection over his length. He is secure in his body, standing before me strong and sure of his sexuality. My lips curve into a soft smile, realizing time has changed so little.

When he moves behind me, I arch my back, pushing my hips toward him, begging with primal body language. *I need you.*

Feeling his strong erection as a caress against my welted thigh, I wiggle my hips. *Take me. Now. Please.*

He leans over me, kissing me gently over the back of my neck and shoulders. His gentleness makes me cry because I have tried so hard over the years not to miss him, not to reminisce about what I shared with him.

I refuse even to consider the consequences of this night or even consider I might still love this man.

"Please, Frankie," I beg, pushing my hips back.

"Please, Frankie?" he asks.

"Please, Master."

He rewards me with a thrust. I gasp. Remembering. John was not well-endowed, and in my naiveté I once thought Frankie was average. Frankie is anything but...

His thrusts are forceful, rough, savage. Pressed against the concrete floor, my flaming, welt-covered ass cheeks welcome the brute honesty of his need. His hand wraps around my middle and his fingers find my clit easily. He remembers my body so well...and I've forgotten so much. I used to come this way for him...I always came for him. I don't climax as he holds me tight and I know he is holding back his own release, waiting for me. I sob, "Please come inside me. Please."

"Not yet," he says.

I scream with frustration, my body responding to the pleasure but refusing to climax. He continues to thrust into me, whispering into my ear in French. I only understand half of what he says, but it is not the words that matter. His voice teases through me, stroking to life all of the forgotten memories I had locked away. He makes me cry. So much time has been lost, time I dare not regret but instead mourn. "Welcome home, Cassiopeia, *maison bienvenue*," he says just before he explodes inside me.

I love the sound Master makes when he comes—half growl, half surprise. When he collapses over me, he is still holding me tightly against him. We fit so well together and I am disappointed I didn't peak. I thought with everything feeling so right I would have...I didn't, I feel robbed. I am disappointed and force my face under control so that how great my disappointment is, is not evident.

"You did not orgasm for me, Cassiopeia."

"No," I whisper.

"When was the last time you had an orgasm?"

"The night you sent me the gift," I answer softly, admitting the truth that I masturbated while wearing the bustier even though such an admission in the past would have brought me intense punishment. I am surprised when he chuckles, rolling me beneath him so I am on my back facing him. "I'm glad you did." He wipes a tear from my cheek and says, "But tonight, you did not surrender yourself to me, and I want to know why."

"I—mm." I close my eyes, there is no hiding the truth, no excuse, so what can I say? I say nothing.

"Open your eyes."

I do as I am told and he gazes long and deep into them, until long after it has become uncomfortable for me to have him keep doing so and I look away.

"It has been a long time since you have allowed yourself to be pleasured by a man?"

I remain silent, not looking him in the face, no excuse sounding appropriate. It isn't that I haven't wondered myself. With John, I stopped having orgasms after I learned he was having affairs, and he stopped having sex with me once he realized I wasn't enjoying him. After the divorce, the two men I dated to whom I was actually attracted enough even to consider getting naked with turned out to be huge disappointments. But Frankie…

Master is not a disappointment.

A sob catches in my throat, making it seem impossible to breathe. I think he feels my desperation because he pulls me up, helping me sit, telling me to "relax" and "just breathe for a moment" as he kneels beside me. Holding me, he strokes me. "What has happened to you over the years?"

"Nothing. Happened," I tell him. I do not know if that is a truth or a lie.

Standing, he pulls me up with him and leads me to a textured wall. Into the wall, eyebolts are attached in an eight-foot diameter. I know without counting there are twelve anchors. Hanging at ten o'clock and two o'clock are iron restraints. "Remember this wall?"

"Yes, Master." I hated this wall, but I don't reveal my feelings to him. I would bet he remembers I did. He jiggles the leather restraint hanging at twelve o'clock, his eyes challenging me, left eyebrow arched with wicked intent. I swallow, mouth dry, armpits suddenly wet. I. Do. Not. Want. To. Be. Restrained. He encourages me. "Come, come."

"It's late," I say.

He chuckles. "You have someplace else to go?"

"No," I squeak.

He does a Vanna White, motioning at the bondage wall with both hands, requesting, "Please?"

I can only stand stunned because he actually used the word please. Oh hell. I step up onto the small platform, not believing I am. I lift my right arm over my head to be cuffed at twelve.

Frankie caresses my wrist and palm before buckling the cuff down tightly, his touch sending need racing through my veins. I'd forgotten this feeling—anxiety, curiosity, impatience. He moves over to the cuff hanging at two o'clock and I lift my left hand. His touch devastates me, leaving me tingling from mere fingertip-strokes over my wrist. Caught, I tug both wrists, knowing I'm not going anywhere.

I am insane…

Two decades could have turned this man into a murderer, I could be in absolute peril at this very moment, but two decades haven't been long enough for me to let go of my complete and absolute trust in this man, so I will soon see how big a mistake I have made.

I watch him as he moves around the room, collecting paraphernalia. Some I recognize, some I don't. He comes toward me, carrying a length of rope, some tubing and a power screwdriver. I fidget, reminding myself I trust him. Telling myself he isn't going to hurt me…or at least won't hurt me so much I can't enjoy the rest. Above all else, Frankie is a sensualist. He wants me to enjoy what he is doing to me.

When he attaches my collar to the board so I lose all neck movement, I start to rethink all of my former reasoning.

The spreader bar he puts between my ankles is an old friend...I just hope he realizes my body probably doesn't bend at the same angles it once did. With the tubing, he makes a sling to help support my hips and thighs, a suspended seat of sorts, then uses the rope to start lifting my legs off the ground. I tell myself I trust him for about the hundredth time as I realize my weight is being supported by tubing and rope. I have already wrapped my hands around the chains, holding the wrist restraints to keep my weight from damaging my joints. I know how this works, he knows what he's doing...

I trust him...

"Relax," he commands.

I laugh because it seems utterly ridiculous I am so tense. I used to love this. *Loved this.*

Yes, yes, I hated the bondage wall...because it was so damn physically taxing, because the process was so damn emotionally taxing, sometimes humiliating, But in the end, when it was all said and done...after I was basking in the post-orgasmic bliss, I admitted to how much I loved it. Hence the impatience for it to be finished.

"You are so beautiful," he tells me and I don't question his view of me. Bound, stretched, uncomfortable...I don't need his words. The look in his eyes tells me how beautiful I am to him. His gaze tells me how much he cherishes me and I can't help but start to cry because John was never able to look at me like that.

I've missed being gazed upon with so much love and need evident.

I belong to Master François Rene de Hart. I always have. I always will.

"What are you thinking?" he asks me.

"Some bonds are eternal."

"Like the one between you and me?" he asks. "*Oui?*"

"Yes," I agree.

He steps beside me, so close his chest pushes into me. He pinches my cheeks between his fingers. "Are you ready to say it yet?"

"Oh god, Frankie," I gasp, self-correcting, "Master. I need time, I need to think…"

I hear the sound of the vibrator, never see it, but know that soon it will be touching me.

"Will you at least come for me, Cassiopeia?" he asks. "Will you trust me to surrender at least that much for me?"

"I'll try."

I feel the vibrator roll along the insides of my thighs. It teases so close to my labia, but does not touch even them.

"Tell me you will surrender to me, Cassiopeia."

I want him to touch me, I need him to touch me, but I don't say what I need to say to guarantee either. I am too honest when I admit, "I don't know if I can."

He surprises me by touching the vibrator to my clit for just a few moments—long enough for heaven to rise up around me—not long enough to peak. He pulls the vibrator away, making me beg, making me gasp.

"Will you surrender to me, Cassiopeia? No more games?"

Why am I being so stubborn? One climax does not mean I am promising to stay forever…

Chapter Four

∞

I awake in his bed, not remembering how I got there, but slowly it all floods back. My screams of pleasure, my screams of pain…but mostly screams making promises by the light of day I'm not so certain I can keep.

* * * * *

"Prostrate yourself to me," Master commanded, releasing my bonds.

I started to rise off the narrow wood table, but he pressed his hand into the middle of my chest, holding me still. "Without sitting up."

I'll fall, my mind screamed. Granted it wasn't far to the tile floor below, but still. I was no longer a spring chicken. I carefully rolled in a tight balancing act, supported at times by only sheer stubbornness and will. I managed to pull back into a fold, precariously balanced on both knees, and push my hands forward until I was in a position of servitude and submission.

"Are you ready to submit to me fully, Charlotte?"

I cringed at the name, longing to hear him call me Cassiopeia. Unable to speak, I nodded.

"Say it." he barked.

"I submit, Master, in all things, in all ways."

Of course we had sex, but then lying on the floor, post-coitus, Master spooned around my backside, me not believing I was there…

I kept waiting to wake up from the dream. This kind of thing just didn't happen to me—*not anymore*. Once maybe…a long time ago…but even that seemed a fantasy, not memory.

"I am glad you returned, Cassiopeia."

He hugged me slightly and I thought he would release me, the hug no more than an announcement to stand or roll over, but it soon became evident he had no intention of either. I was confused, because Master was never a snuggler, but then his erection pressed into my hip and the message became more clear. *Really? Again?* I was exhausted. He had to be as well. But how could I even imagine wanting to sleep when I was there in his arms?

No, I knew there would be no sleeping until I was home in my own bed…

Only then would I have time to process all of this. But even then, I knew I wouldn't sleep.

I thought about my daughters. *God, this is not soccer mom behavior.*

"Your thoughts are troubled," he says.

"I can't believe I'm here."

"But here you are and that makes me very glad. Are you too glad? Or is it regret that troubles you?"

I rolled onto my back and looked into his face. *Master.* I stroked his jaw, so glad my hands were free and I could finally touch him. "Not regret. Disbelief, maybe, that I returned so easily…dropped to my knees at the train station…fell in almost where we left off. It all seems so impossibly easy to be Cassiopeia again. I guess I'm waiting to wake up."

"You are quite awake."

"Or waiting for the other shoe to drop."

He smirked. "I have never understood that phrase."

"It can't be this perfect. Something will happen to mess this up."

"Have you always been such a pessimist?"

I sighed, sounding more frustrated and unhappy than I intended. I was happy. Deliriously so.

I knew he was going to kiss me even before his head dropped to do so. The tenderness of his lips after such intense passion only moments ago brought tears to my eyes and it suddenly seemed I couldn't breathe, my chest was so congested with emotion.

He pulled away, meeting my gaze.

"I can't be sorry I left. My girls—"

He pressed his finger to my lips. "I don't want you to be sorry."

New emotion flooded through my veins and I lay caught between hyperventilating and crying. My heart thudded in my chest, threatening to break free as I admitted, "I never stopped loving you. Not for a single moment."

When his mouth claimed mine again, there was no tenderness, just raw passion. His body covered mine and my legs wrapped around his hips.

We were meant for this, he and I.

There was no awkwardness as our bodies joined, no fumbling to make his parts meld with mine. *John.* I pushed the unwanted thought of my ex away. There was no rental space left in my brain for him now. My heart and mind had room for only one. Master.

Our rhythm was perfect and my body responded, embarrassingly fast.

"Ahhh!"

"*Oui.* Give me your pleasure. I want to feel the flood of you covering me." He kissed my eyelids, my nose, my brow. His thrusts became more sure, more determined. He pounded my orgasm out of me and I was left screaming his name, and obscenities, and *I love you.*

"I love you too, Cassiopeia. Promise you will stay. Promise you will never leave me again."

His thrusts pushed emotion deeper and deeper into my soul. I cried out his name again. Couldn't he see he was killing me emotionally?

I couldn't make that commitment.

I couldn't...

"Promise me."

"I promise. I will never leave you again. I love you. I love you."

And then the other shoe dropped.

We left the dungeon and he gave me the grand tour of the house. It hadn't changed too much, a new couch in the main parlor, a new rug in the dining room, and a new house slave busy polishing silverware in the kitchen. He was young. No, not coed young. Maybe twenty-five, not-yet-thirty young...but holy mother of god beautiful...and as naked as I.

"Cassiopeia, this is Pierre-Louis Lefèvre."

He stood and I immediately blushed, humiliated I had looked *there*, but how could I not look when he looked like that. Damn. Good. I was ashamed, especially after only moments before thinking how well Frankie was wearing his age...how sexy he was despite his graying temples and his extra few pounds. I couldn't stop looking at Pierre-Louis, and though my brain was screaming at me to look away... God, yes, I kept looking...and the house slave looked back at me without censure. Since when were house slaves allowed to have their eyes anywhere except on the floor?

It seemed to me Pierre-Louis Lefèvre was overly bold, but it was not my place to take action against him, and obviously Master had no intention of correcting his behavior. I wondered what his slave thought seeing me there, obviously the recent recipient of Master's attention, as evidenced by my many welts and bruises. I had forgotten the pride connected to wearing another's mark.

Embracing my pride, I'd lifted my chin a notch and locked gazes with the man. A flashback of memory erupted in my brain at the wrong moment for me to remain too arrogant though. I remembered how it felt to be in his place, serving Master and another, wondering what I had done wrong to deserve such treatment as to be replaced and knowing the answer was nothing. Master could keep me, use me, replace me at will. My heart would be breaking in two as I watched Master caress the other...and the other wouldn't even acknowledge my existence.

I acknowledged him. No, I didn't stick out my hand to shake along with the introductions, but I did soften my gaze from one of competition and hostility to one of acceptance and equality. I hitched my chin up as I said "Hello," and smiled, wondering how long Pierre-Louis would be sticking around. If I was lucky, he would finish doing his tasks quickly and be dismissed. It never dawned on me he might actually be staying.

Behind me, Master chuckled. "I'm glad you approve. I would hate to have to ask Pierre-Louis to move out."

"He lives here?" I croaked.

"*Oui,*" he says. "He lives here. With me."

Fortunately we stood near the kitchen table and I sat in the nearest chair to keep from falling. Pierre-Louis is me twenty years ago. Except he won't leave because his biological clock is ticking.

I looked between the two men, my gaze finally meeting Master's. *Do you love him?*

How can I even wonder that? It's obvious he does.

Make him move out. This wasn't part of the Cassiopeia Comeback.

I was still looking though, tongue not working, but how could I not look? The two men were opposites. Whereas Frankie was dark, Pierre-Louis was fair, his blond hair cut almost military short, his blue eyes the color of a brilliant winter sky...and he was tall, several inches taller than Frankie...and more muscular than Frankie. The man was a walking wet dream from the top of his tow head to the tips of his perfectly bare toes. As I watched, Pierre-Louis went to the wine closet and retrieved three bottles of French Bordeaux. Without being asked he started uncorking and filling glasses with the deep ruby liquid. I accepted a glass and very unsophisticatedly downed the contents in one long swallow — no sniffing, no swishing, just swallowing before holding the glass back out to him. He kindly poured more without comment. When he handed me the glass our fingertips touched. A zap of electricity wouldn't have been more powerful. My world shattered in that moment.

I am still Cassiopeia.

Where have I been hiding all of these years? I thought I'd stayed the same person...but clearly I haven't. I've kept myself, my need, tightly reined in. I allowed myself to forget want, need, desire. Lust. It was an odd realization. My sex drive hadn't died with my marriage.

Maybe it only went dormant for a little while, because being across the room from Frankie and Pierre-Louis, I was filled with a lust greater than any I'd ever known before, and I gave myself permission to feel it. The woman I was yesterday would have shuttered it back behind some false propriety, some suburban morality. Cassiopeia had no such codes.

I wanted to ask Frankie what he was thinking. I knew what I was thinking. Or rather, what I was refusing to admit I was thinking — because what I was thinking was too obscene. I was wondering what it would feel like to wrap my nakedness around the lean, firm body of a young man in his prime. And I didn't even feel dirty thinking it. Pierre-Louis looked as though he was born to fuck. I was thinking I couldn't wait for the real games to begin with Master...

Yes, yes, at home in my bedroom I barely allowed myself to remember the pony games, but there were other games, days of game after game when the manse would become orgy central. If I'd have remembered *that* I wouldn't have been brave enough to have returned.

Master wouldn't share me, not for sex, but other men, and women too, could spank me, humiliate me…kiss me.

Looking at Pierre-Louis, well, I could begin to imagine, and I wouldn't want it to end with kissing.

Frankie sat down at the table, as did Pierre-Louis. Sitting nude at the table, we drank wine and Pierre-Louis was forward enough to start talking, his thick French accent making all of my nerve endings tingle. "I have been so desperate to meet you."

My eyebrow rose at his admission.

"Master has told me so much about the old days."

The *old* days? Obviously, Pierre-Louis talked too much…

* * * * *

I turn my head to face Frankie and find he is awake too.

He reaches out to touch my face. "You're still here."

I smile. "I have no idea why. Last night was —"

"Incredible?" Frankie asks.

"I was thinking humiliating."

"You enjoyed yourself. I'd forgotten what a naughty flirt you could be."

"Oh god, I had sex with him?"

"No, not yet."

"Thank god." I bury my face in my hands, doubly embarrassed I considered it could have happened, and Frankie believes at some point it will happen. For now I am thankful the images filling my brain are just the memory of an erotic dream caused by too much adrenaline, too much Bordeaux and two sexy men. I know I'm projecting my own insecurities on to Frankie when I accuse, "He's too young for you."

"No. I am French. Too young for your American mind."

49

"Too young for my American body," I say vehemently, feeling angry and jealous and hungover. *What was I thinking last night? Orgy? Really?*

Frankie smiles and caresses my breast. "Your body is beautiful and because of how sexy you are, poor Pierre-Louis had an erection all evening."

I sigh, not wanting to admit I'd noticed and, had I been twenty years younger I would have done more than merely looked. I demand, "What are you thinking? It was going to be hard enough to tell my daughters, 'Welcome to Mom's new kinky life.' How will I ever admit to them, 'This is my Master, François, and this is his lover, Pierre-Louis. Maybe you know him from school?'"

Frankie laughs loudly and pulls me tightly into his arms. "Your children will know only as much or as little as you want them to know and if it will make you feel any better, Pierre-Louis is twenty-eight."

"Oh god."

"What?"

"I'm sixteen years older than he is."

"So?" he asks. "And it's seventeen, you had a birthday, remember?"

I shake my head, trying to say the words that this is impossible, but I want it to be possible. I want to be the Cassiopeia I remember being. A tap at the door startles me.

"*Oui? Entre.*"

The door opens and still-nude Pierre-Louis enters bearing a tray, shiny domes hiding what I assume is breakfast. He sets the tray on a table and throws open the double doors to the balconied terrace before motioning us to join him outside. He carries the tray out and sets the table. I look at Frankie, my vision a little blurred around the edges. Am I dreaming? Will I wake up in my own bed, another day older but otherwise unchanged?

Frankie rises and pulls on a gray silk robe. I sit up and the weight of my collar is heavy around my neck. I watch as Frankie joins Pierre-Louis on the balcony. He kisses his cheek and whispers softly to him in French, "*Merci. C'est magnifique.*" Their kiss becomes more intimate and I watch, unable to turn away even when Frankie whispers, "*Je t'aime,*" against Pierre-Louis' cheek.

My ringing cell phone draws my attention to my purse. I don't think not to answer, my children are in a foreign country, and today I don't even know which one. In the back of my mind the thought is there that the Cassiopeia of old would have asked permission to make or answer a call. Oh hell. The Cassiopeia of old did not have a job...or children. "Hello?"

"Mommeee."

"Bree." I smile saying her name.

"Did we wake you? I know it's Saturday morning and you like to sleep in, but we're boarding a ship in two days and I want you to know the plan because the itinerary is a little complicated."

A plan? My parents have a plan, including a boat and an itinerary?

Concern knots my middle and I sit on the edge of the bed, bracing myself, trying to sound calm as I ask, "Where are you today?"

"Rome," she answers excitedly, gushing, "It's amazing here. I may never want to come home."

My stomach flip-flops.

"J.K.," she says, laughing. My mommy brain translates, *just kidding*. I manage to say, "Ha ha."

Bree admits, "I miss you terribly. Are you horribly lonely without us?"

I look at the two men on the balcony before turning my back to them, hoping to stop the flood of desire for the sexual odyssey I have only to accept to embark on. I tell my daughter, "I miss you terribly."

"Good. I'd hate to think you were out painting the town red like Daddy is. Have you talked to him? Wow. How do you spell mid-life crisis? Freshman. Hello? But you did not hear that from me."

I titter nervously, eyeing Pierre-Louis. "Really? I suppose she's a redhead."

"Ick." I feel her disgust then, without changing tone she says, "Anyway, your other child is demanding I share the phone."

Uh-oh. The girls are fighting. Marvelous.

"Hi, Mom." Ellie is tightly restrained.

"Hi yourself, kiddo. What's going on?"

"I hate men. All men. I don't know how you ever put up with one long enough to conceive us." I peek over my shoulder at Master and Pierre-Louis.

"Not all men are horrible." I watch as Pierre-Louis lifts the shiny domes from the plates. He looks up and beckons me out. I shake my head and lift a finger signaling I need a moment.

"Bree mentioned a travel plan?"

"Yes," she says, her misery evident in just one word. "A plan."

I decide she sounds a bit like Eeyore from the *Winnie the Pooh* movie we watched to death when she was young. "God, Ellie, you sound miserable. Do you want to fly home? Because you can come home." My heart is true as I make the promise, but an evil part of me hopes she really doesn't want to come home because I'd really like to make some plans of my own and all of them are too X-rated to let my teen daughter know about.

"No. I'm fine."

I sigh, relieved. Her imminent return delayed at least a little while. "If I'm going to be miserable I might as well be miserable in the most exotic locations on the planet."

Definitely Eeyore. "Oh, baby," I say, pouting. "I wish there was something I could do. Maybe you could do something for me?"

"Okay?" She answers suspiciously and I think for a moment she is concerned I am going to ask if it is okay for me to join them. I rub my face. I am more dreaded than the misery of lost love. When did my children start seeing me as a killjoy?

"Can you start a blog about your adventures? Then I won't have to wait until you get home to see the places you are seeing."

"Oh. Excellent." Her voice brightens considerably. "Why didn't we think of this before we left? I have so much to do just to get a page caught up from when we started to now. I've lost an entire week. Oh, Mom. Thank you. I'll send you a link. Here's Grandpa. I love you."

I hear the phone clatter. "Bree? Dad? Ellie?"

My dad's voice comes over the receiver. "I'm here. I'm here. I don't know what you said to her, but she's smiling for the first time since leaving Amsterdam. Thank you."

"You should have had her call sooner."

He laughs and it is good to hear my dad do so. "Trust me, next time I will. I think I'm getting too old to deal with teen girl hormones."

Now I laugh. "Welcome to my world." I turn completely around to see what the men on the balcony are up to. Biting my lip, I gather courage to berate my dad about the girls' trip to the discothèque and subsequent alcohol usage. And the brownies...

My head tilts as I watch Pierre-Louis pour mimosa into Frankie's glass. Muscles flex in his arm and chest I didn't even know men had. He smiles at Frankie, Frankie smiles back and I shake my head, remembering I am here to enjoy Frankie. Pierre-Louis is just eye candy, that's all.

My dad volunteers, "The brownies didn't have any marijuana in them. I wanted you to know that. I made certain. You have enough to worry about with your girls out of the country and without being stressed about that too."

"Wow," I say, slightly stunned. "I appreciate your honesty…but there was some alcohol involved later that evening, I believe…and so I was still worried."

He sighs. I know he wants this fight even less than I do. I can see him nodding his head in my mind, his face twisted trying to figure out what he can say that won't piss me off. I talk when he doesn't say anything, "Look, just keep them safe. Whether they are at a frat house next fall or in Europe with you, I know teenagers, and given an inch…"

He laughs. "They'll take a mile. I'll keep them safe, Charley. Don't worry."

"Great," I say, feeling a little better but not completely relieved of worry. I ask, "Itinerary?"

"It's a bit complicated."

"Maybe you should email it to me."

"We already did. Haven't you checked your email?"

Guiltily, I look at the two distractions currently watching me from the balcony. "My server was down yesterday. I can open it today…" I catch the kiss Frankie blows to me and smile at him. "Hopefully."

"Good, good. Look, here's the quick rundown. We're doing a bit of a Mediterranean cruise. All the big cities and some small ones. They're all on the list."

"What aren't you telling me?"

"Nothing, nothing. I want the girls to see every place I possibly can show them. Just the normal places, Dubrovnik, Bari, Piraeus, Kirkira Corfu, Istanbul, Katakolon. And maybe a side venture or two."

My kids-in-danger Mommy-radar flashes on high alert. "Dad? Where else?"

"We might arrange a private tour from Marrakech to Casablanca, pass through Tinghir, Fez."

My mouth drops. "Isn't Marrakech dangerous? This doesn't sound like any cruise I've heard of."

"Completely safe. I've rented a vessel and the political climate is fairly calm right now. I wouldn't take the girls if I couldn't guarantee their safety. And when have I ever taken a typical route anywhere?"

True. "You are not a typical guy, Dad." My unease spikes. "You rented a vessel? Who's piloting the vessel?"

"Not me." He laughs. "We have a crew and twenty-three ports of call."

"Sounds ambitious." I frown, thinking I'm glad it's him and not me. As lovely as a trip cruising around the sunny, exotic Mediterranean sounds, I've lived long enough to know the high seas and I don't fare well together. I would be the one with my head hanging over a toilet the entire trip. "It sounds like a great time, Dad. I'm glad you could do this for Ells and Bree."

"Love you, girl. We'll call again soon."

Click.

"Dad?" I say his name even though I am fairly sure he hung up. I shake my head and, keeping my cell in my hand just in case one of the girls calls back, I join the men on the balcony. My distress must be evident on my face because both Frankie and Pierre-Louis look at me sympathetically. Frankie asks, "All fine on the home front?"

"Time will tell," I answer.

I am naked except for the collar, and strangely unselfconscious. It is an odd moment though, when Frankie pulls out a chair for me. Both the table and chairs are ornate wrought iron but the chairs are fitted with thick, soft cushions. My reaction must be readable upon my face because Frankie explains, "We're not as young as we used to be, and I don't expect you to kneel at my feet." I nod and take a seat, although I am not sure whether I am relieved or disappointed. Obviously, regardless of age and virility, Pierre-Louis has been sitting on a seat and eating beside him. Much has changed since I was here.

Standing, Pierre-Louis grabs my plate. "I'll reheat everything and make you fresh eggs. These are cold."

I touch his wrist and our gazes meet. I jerk my eyes from his, not liking feeling what looking into his eyes makes me feel. "They're fine. I've eaten a lot of cold eggs in my lifetime."

He takes my plate away anyway, saying, "It'll just take a moment."

I look at Frankie and he looks like a cat that just ate the cream. "What?"

"Just enjoying watching you squirm."

I lift my chin, denying his assessment. "I have no idea what you are talking about."

"Sure you do. When's the last time you felt lust like that?"

"Last night. With. You," I answer, making him roar with laughter.

"Lust for me?" he says coyly, "*Oui*. And I for you, including every day we have been apart. I want you. I need you. I adore you. But. Him? The lust you felt for him was an entirely different animal, and I will not be hurt if you admit the truth. So, I ask again, when was the last time you felt lust as you felt for Pierre-Louis last night?"

I square my jaw and grind my teeth before admitting, "Maybe never. No offense, because you are beautiful, and you've always been beautiful..."

"But I couldn't have competed with him even when I was twenty-eight," he admits with a chuckle.

I can't believe this is the same Frankie. I cannot believe I have been away so long. It seems as if I haven't been away...or that it was just yesterday. I cannot take my eyes off him, he is so beautiful to me and it amazes me I was ever strong enough to walk away from him.

He volunteers, "Pierre-Louis is a fuck machine. I want you to know the pleasure he can give you. I want you to know the mind-blowing joy we can give you."

"We?" I demand. "As in the both of you…with me…together? At the same time?" I sound shrill and offended even to my own ears, but the evil seed has been planted and the vision of what could be explodes through my mind. "Why are you doing this to me? Wasn't it enough of a mind-fuck for you to summon me after almost two decades?"

"This isn't a mental game, Cassiopeia. This is my life now. Pierre-Louis is part of my life and I want you to be part of my life. The only way I see of making this work is for us to form a ménage."

"No."

"You want him."

I laugh at the cruelty of the situation, and my laugh comes out cold and bitter. "I'm old, François. That young man isn't going to want me."

"You never did realize how sensual you were."

"Key word. Were. Was. Not anymore."

"Still. More so now than ever before. You have finally grown into your body."

I sputter, wondering what in the hell that means. He spears a link of sausage and deftly changes the subject. "How are your daughters today?"

"Oh shit," I say, coming to my senses, remembering my conversation with my father. "Do you know anything about the political climate of Marrakech? Or Algiers? It seems there's been a change of plans. Europe is over and done and the Mediterranean is on."

Frankie pats my hand. "I'm sure they will be fine, but I'll make some calls after breakfast." His gaze doesn't leave mine as he adds, "We could always join them if it would make you feel better."

"Join them? I have work on Monday. I—" Why am I blaming work, when it isn't work at all? Because if it was only work, I would have already been on the plane. The objection is the *we* and not even the we as in me and Frankie. I might actually be able to face my girls if it was just him. But when Frankie said we, I knew he meant all of us...and that I don't think I'll ever be ready for. I sigh, facing the truth. "As wonderful as it has been, seeing you again, I still don't know how this," I gesture at my nudity and collar, "will ever coexist with my real life."

"This is your real life now." Frankie shakes his head, his lips twitching. "I will assist you in any way I can to maintain a charade of propriety while in the company of your children, but my slaves don't work...at least not outside the home. You will quit."

Pierre-Louis returns with fresh eggs and sits. I stand, shaking, sputtering. "I'm—I—What do you think—? Who do you think you are? I do work. I have a career. I cannot just give up everything on a moment's notice."

Too late I see the flash of hurt in his eyes, the discomfort in Pierre-Louis' eyes. Of course he probably knows the story. I left. Without any warning. I just left. He does not have to say "Once you did" for me to feel the sting. Silence would have been enough. What am I doing? What?

I sit back down and stare at my eggs. They are perfectly prepared, over easy but flipped, an almost impossible task. And Pierre-Louis accomplished it not once this morning but twice. I let out the breath I didn't realize I'd been holding. "Thank you for the eggs, they're perfect."

I manage to make eye contact with Frankie. I don't know how, but I do. "I've never apologized."

"An apology is unnecessary unless you are leaving me again."

I shake my head, a tear sliding down my cheek, my heart lodged in my throat. I cannot imagine walking away from this man a second time. "Help me make this work."

"*Oui*," he says. "I will help you. You must do your part."

"How? By giving up my job? What next? My home? My car? My bank accounts?" I start to panic and the terror is evident in my voice.

"We begin with breakfast. Eat."

"Eat? When I have no idea how to do what you are asking me to do?"

"I am only asking for your unconditional surrender. After that, everything is simple."

I start to laugh hysterically. "Simple. Sure." I take a bite of eggs and am surprised at how wonderful they are, how hungry I am, and can't quite believe I am able to eat at all under the circumstances. "I realize how easy that is for you to say."

"*Au contraire*," he says. "Asking you to return to me is the hardest thing I have ever done."

The emotion I hear in his voice makes me look up at him. "Frankie."

"I died a little when you left me. You and I are bound, Cassiopeia."

Yes, I feel that.

"I do not want your house or car or bank accounts. I do not want to interfere with your relationship with your children."

The offense I hear in his voice rips through my chest.

"I want you in my life—every second of every minute of every hour. I will not compete with a nine-to-five job when you have already stolen years from me." His gaze burns through me, making me shake, not with fear but with need.

Anger makes him growl "years" as his fist hits the table, shaking the china and silverware. I jerk in my seat, wishing I could take back the pain I caused him but unable to wish away the time I spent without him. I understand. I wish I didn't but I do. I wish I could come back to reason but I don't believe I am insane. I realize without a doubt I want this too.

"Is two weeks' notice acceptable?" I ask.

"If you use your two weeks in vacation time, *oui*."

I nod, knowing that won't be a problem. It also isn't much of a risk because my employer loves me and would take me back in a single heartbeat if everything fell apart. I don't tell him any of that. I just sit, nodding, accepting, letting it soak in that I am willing to do this. Unconditional surrender. I didn't realize it was a war. I wave my white flag, saying, "As you wish, Master." It sounds so corny in my head, and I wonder if it ever really sounded normal when I said it before. I hope it starts to feel normal soon so I won't be tempted to giggle, because there isn't anything funny about what is transpiring between us.

This is not a game. This is his life. And now, again, my life too.

He nods, returning his attention to the fresh fruit on his plate.

"I will need you to gather some things from your house. Your passport and other important documents."

I sit in stunned silence, my mouth opening and closing like a goldfish. He spears a bite-sized piece of melon on his fork. "You do wish to at least be in the same time zone as your children, *oui*? That will give you some peace of mind?"

I nod.

"Good, because I do not want to see worry etched across your face every minute of every day we are together. Pain? *Oui*. Orgasmic pleasure? Most certainly. But worry is not acceptable, and we have much to do if we are going to create a bond between the three of us."

He speaks as if we are sitting in a boardroom discussing deadlines and quotas, not relationships that involve people and emotions. I look at Pierre-Louis, but his gaze too is on Frankie. There is no panic or worry in his gaze, there is just absolute trust. I take a deep breath, remembering when I used to gaze upon Frankie with such reverence. I'm not sure I can ever place him…any man…back on such a high pedestal ever again.

I hate that I've lost my trust, become so jaded…trust and surrender were once so much easier than anything I have ever done since.

"You want all of us to go to France?"

"*Oui*," he answers, lifting his cup of coffee to his lips.

"To Saint-Émilion?"

"Of course."

Yes, of course. I suppose if you are the owner of a château in the Burgundy wine country, it would only make sense to stay there when in the country. I bite down on my lip, making certain a single sound doesn't come out of my mouth because I cannot trust what the sound would be. Frustration? Elation? Exasperation?

He is taking over my life where we left off. Quit your job. Pfft. *Seriously?* We are going to France. Where we once planned to grow old together. My heart still aches over that lost dream.

How in the hell do we do this? How do I do this?

Chapter Five

ഇ

Passports in order all around definitely make leaving the country at a moment's notice easier, as far as logistics go, anyway. However, a piece of myself is still back at my house in Glenview. Frankie drove me there to pack. Unreal isn't the right word, neither is surreal, although both words could be used to explain what it felt like to have Frankie in my house. In. My. House.

I wore a trench coat and four-inch heels home, not so exceptional given it was raining cats and dogs. What was bizarre was the fact I was completely naked beneath the long coat except for my leather collar, and as soon as we crossed the threshold Frankie helped me out of the coat, leaving me standing in my foyer naked. My heart was racing so fast I thought I might stroke out, which left me shattered, shaking. I thought, *if this is a dream, I need to wake up now. Now.*

I didn't wake up.

He said, "Thirty minutes, Cassiopeia. Pack everything you need for an extended stay in France."

"Extended?" I asked, panicked.

"You did say the girls are staying away the entire summer, yes?"

I nodded, still dazed, having no idea what to pack.

He seemed to understand my conundrum because he suggested, "Several dresses, some slacks and blouses. Any toiletries beyond a few days' time can be purchased there. Do you have a favorite photograph of the girls, perhaps? Hair dryer? Curling iron? Hair straightener? Makeup?"

I awakened inside the insanity of the moment. "Okay, okay. I get it."

Walking through my house wearing only my stilettos and collar, I felt like a complete stranger. The house seemed all wrong, even though I remembered the best and worst moments each room had to offer, the ghosts of happiness and sadness, dreams both accomplished and forgotten. I reached the bedroom once shared by John and me, wishing I had known more joy in the room and less desolation. I caught my reflection in the long dressing mirror and turned to look at the bruises striping my ass and thighs from the caning. It seemed strange to see bruises on my ass in that mirror.

Was the caning only last night? Really?

It felt as if I'd been away from home for weeks, maybe months, my disorientation was so complete.

I closed my eyes, remembering how many nights I'd wished I could admit to John my needs that he wasn't able to meet. It wasn't that he was a horrible fuck, I just needed more than the casual, emotionless sex he was able to provide. It wasn't hard to start packing after seeing my past through Cassiopeia's eyes.

Am I mentally ill because I am dissociating? I shouldn't feel as if I am two distinct people...two distinct lives...and I wonder again how my two selves, my two lives, will ever merge.

And now I sit between two men, twenty thousand feet above the ground.

One I fucked last night.

One I will fuck tonight.

Of that I have no doubt as I begin this new journey, this new era of my life. I think Frankie is a genius. I could never have started a relationship with Pierre-Louis at the manor where I originally fell in love with Master. I could never have recreated with Frankie what we once shared if I was coming and going between the home I raised my children in, the manor and my job. In France we have the chance of doing both, and I am left feeling optimistic.

We are flying in Frankie's private jet. I'd forgotten the perks of being with him—no commercial flights, meaning no crying children, no prying eyes. We can do as we wish...

I chance a shy look at Pierre-Louis and he catches me looking. He smiles and winks, making me blush, and beside me Frankie chuckles. My mind fills with thoughts and images better saved for when we are on the ground, but honestly I want to know how it will feel to have both men touching me at the same time and I don't know if I can wait until the plane touches down to find out.

I cast my eyes down to my lap. Safe territory. Relatively safe at least. Not looking at either man. Interestingly, I am wearing dark indigo jeans with rhinestone details I fell in love with at the department store but never had an occasion to wear. A last-minute flight to France seemed a good enough excuse. Likewise, the black sleeveless shell is a clearance find by Eileen Fisher and even at its discounted price seemed too extravagant for a mere workday, but paired with five-inch-heeled, black leather, lace-front slingbacks imported from Italy—another clearance find—also never worn, is perfect for this trip. Besides, the leather collar almost looks like a fashion accessory. Almost.

Even though I am clothed, making it a safer trip through airport security, I feel naughty, giddily so.

I could feel heads turning as I walked through the terminal, eyes looking, both men and women. I didn't feel any condemnation, no pointing and laughing, just appreciation for a beautiful woman. Damn. I'd forgotten how that felt. To remember I was once beautiful and to feel beautiful again.

There is no way to describe the feeling other than gratitude. I am so glad for this moment in time, so thankful.

Frankie reaches over, expecting me to take hold of his hand. I do, glad when I feel him squeeze my fingers. I look up at him and smile, wondering if he can guess my thoughts. He leans over and whispers, "Poor Pierre-Louis is drooling over you. Kiss him."

My lips part to refuse, but then I remember the rule, one doesn't refuse anything Master asks. I lift my eyebrows, hoping I heard him correctly, worried I didn't, but then he encourages, "Go ahead, do it now."

I feel my eyes go wide. I have no idea what I'm doing as I turn to face Pierre-Louis. He looks at me expectantly, making me wonder if he overheard. He lifts his eyebrow questioningly, making me think he didn't overhear. Frankie releases his hold on my hand and I giggle self-consciously. I fidget in my seat so I am facing more toward Pierre-Louis, with my back slightly toward Frankie. I think I should tell him what I plan. I have been commanded to kiss him. But then his light-blue eyes brighten and as my mouth moves, trying to say something but not succeeding, he tilts his head and I know if I only lean in our lips will collide. Then surely one or both of us will figure it out from there, right?

I lean in and, with a nudge in the center of my back from Frankie, our lips do touch, but it isn't exactly a kiss. He is looking at me, I am looking at him, our gazes catching, his breath warm and sweet on my face, and I realize I have to do this. I reach my hand up to stroke his cheek, the same hand that just moments ago was holding Frankie's, but I try not to think about it.

It's impossible not to think about.

I stroke Pierre-Louis' cheek, pressing my lips closer until they are flat against his and I am feeling awkward. Oh hell. His lips move beneath mine and mine move with his until we are really kissing and the uneasiness vanishes within the workings of his expertise.

His tongue slides along my bottom lip, begging access to my mouth, and I grant him entrance, allowing our tongues to play. The entire time my brain is on overload. I'm still thinking.

Thinking too much.

Worrying. About everything.

Frankie wants a ménage, but Pierre-Louis is so young, or maybe I am just too old, and what would happen if my daughters discovered our secret, and holy fuck, I've already decided to have sex with him, because if he grinds as well as he kisses… Holy. Mother. Of. God.

"Yes," he answers.

"Yes?" I ask into his mouth, confused.

"You wanted to know if I fuck as well as I kiss," he says, his French accent as much a turn-on as the rest of him, just as Frankie's brogue ever did it for me. Dear god, how will I ever stand two French men whispering sweet nothings into my ear in their pleasantly exotic voices?

"I did?" I ask, mesmerized by his gaze. I wonder if he shouts in French when he orgasms.

He chuckles. "You just asked me."

I sit back, horrified. "I didn't."

He winks, laughing. "You didn't but you did wonder, *oui*?"

I cover my mouth with my hand, hiding my own laughter. Embarrassed. He doesn't need to know the answer to that.

The pilot announces, "We have just left US airspace."

God, this is going to be a long flight.

He holds out his hand to me. "Come here?"

"Here?" I ask, suddenly panicked.

He pats his knee. "*Oui*, here."

My heart flutters wildly in my chest. I have no idea what is expected or by whom. Frankie tops me, no one else ever has, and Pierre-Louis bottoms to Frankie, but will he be allowed to top me? Master's lack of interference in the situation seems to denote yes, he might actually allow Pierre-Louis to top me. God, how do I feel about that?

Do I actually see myself topping him? Well, maybe. It might be fun. God, oh god. I don't know what to do. He sits, waiting patiently, watching me.

I can only assume I look as panicked as I feel.

He shrugs and challenges with his gaze, looking so masculine, so predatory...and laughing. His gaze absolutely holds laughter. At me? With me?

I'm not laughing.

Frankie leans into my back, resting his chin on my shoulder. He whispers, "Are you afraid? Are you awaiting my permission?"

I turn my head and see the same challenging smirk on his face.

"I want you to enjoy him," he says. "There is time for roles later. No topping, no bottoming, just you and him, exploring each other. Get to know him."

Get to know him? Intimately, right? Not just chatting? I swallow hard, trapped between the laughter of two men, feeling completely out of my league. What am I doing here? On this plane? I should be at work. I should be...bored out of my mind right now.

No. I've spent long enough being good. Is that what I've been doing as part of the normal, vanilla world? Being good? While my philandering husband screwed coeds? I push down my anger, not helpful on this trip, but still feel guilt. I have responsibilities to others. Like my children. Am I seriously considering what they don't know about Mommy won't hurt them?

I push back against Frankie. "This isn't as easy for me as it was when I was twenty-something."

He kisses the side of my face and a thrill of pleasure speeds through my veins.

"I never expected it to be easy. I do assume you still desire to please me above all else though."

Damn. Do I?

Fuck.

I. Am. Not. The. Same. Person.

"Sit in his lap. What can it hurt? You have your clothes on, he has his clothing on. Get to know him better. It is easier this way than forced nude together in the backseat as we drive through the country to the estate, am I wrong?"

Oh god. Easier. Yes.

I stand, pivot and sit my ass on Pierre-Louis' knee. I feel awkward. I let out a deep breath, not looking at either man as I try to draw from a reserve of fortitude. This is every woman's dream, right? I should be doing cartwheels over the opportunity. I glance up, not at Frankie. Looking at Frankie this second would be too much. I lock on Pierre-Louis' gaze and don't find laughter or teasing. I find patience. Perhaps even empathy. He runs his hands up my back in a gentle caress, easing his fingers into my tense shoulder muscles when he finds them strung tight. He rubs softly, not sensually, and that is good. He is sexy enough and it is difficult already, sitting in his lap, without him trying to seduce.

Massaging harder, he elicits deep appreciation, though I don't say it. I think he realizes. I lose track of time when he turns me so both of his hands can knead and rub. I am content, my eyes closed, and when I feel him pulling me back against his chest, I stiffen a little. He molds his body into mine. "Sh-sh-sh, relax," he says, his arms going around to hold me close to him. "Just getting to know one another, *oui*?"

I don't open my eyes, and do the best I can to let the tension run out of my limbs. His hands roam over my stomach and ribs, making me self-conscious of the extra twenty pounds, but then he wouldn't know that, only Frankie would know.

I move my hands over his, catching his wrists and pulling so his arms and mine are crossed over my stomach. His fingers play over my ribs and I'm okay with that. Not one hundred percent comfortable, but better.

He kisses the side of my face and I think he seems more mature than twenty-eight, his patience earning him bonus points. I think we should have gotten all of this getting to know each other stuff out of the way when I was drunk on Bordeaux, but then I wouldn't remember and I would still be just as awkward.

He slides his hand under the edge of my shirt to find bare skin. The warm touch is startling. Hot against my skin. No way to escape the sensation of so much heat traveling over my flesh, rubbing my stomach, teasing my ribs. His other hand joins the first, both roaming, and I am at a loss with what to do with mine even though they are resting on my thighs. It seems I should be doing something, touching him. Stopping him. I don't move, keeping my own hands where they are and relaxing into the sensation of him touching me, his caress exquisite. And sensual.

I don't think about the *what next*. I just stay wrapped in the delight his fingers are causing my flesh. I appreciate that his touch doesn't stray to my breasts or *lower*, and I am grateful he is consciously giving me time to get used to him, but then after a while I want him to explore my womanly places. I pray he won't make me ask, or worse, beg. I arch my back, moving my hips, and he pushes me forward, staying molded around me, readjusting us. My head drops forward, exposing the long line of my neck to him as my hair shifts with the motion. I feel limp as a dishrag but oh so horny. He doesn't disappoint me, dropping a line of kisses over the back of my neck that leaves me trembling. I realize only after a moment of lost-in-space utter pleasure that he is unbuttoning and unzipping my jeans. He adjusts my body backward, taking my shirt by the tail and tugging it over my head in a smooth move. I gasp but he doesn't stop. He holds me tight around the waist and I see Frankie has already knelt and is unbuckling my sandals. Once my shoes are off, he pulls down my pants.

The cabin of the jet suddenly seems chilly as I recline against Pierre-Louis' warmth in my lace bra and panties.

Without a word Frankie returns to his seat. To. Watch. Oh shit.

Pierre-Louis kisses my shoulder, my neck. Watching Frankie watching reminds me of the past, parties he would allow me to participate in only so much—dangling me like a ripe cherry perhaps—before pulling me away. It makes me feel strange that he has actually suggested a ménage, implied Pierre-Louis and I will be lovers. I wonder if I will watch the two of them do more than kiss. I wonder—even though I know Frankie tops and Pierre-Louis bottoms in their relationship—who actually does whom in the bedroom. I feel myself blushing. These are not thoughts I should be having right now.

Pierre-Louis slides his hand beneath the waistband of my lace panties and suddenly my attention is diverted back to the man whose lap I sit in. I turn my head to look at the man touching me instead of the man watching us. His blue eyes flash at me, making me feel he is glad he has my undivided attention again. He teasingly nips my shoulder, a slight distraction to take my mind off his fingers traveling deeper inside my panties. Does he really think he can take my mind off realizing he is finding me slippery and ready? His fingers tease through my folds and my hips respond with small rocks against his thigh.

I never dreamed anything like this would ever happen. Even after the gift from Frankie, even after my mind adjusted to the thought I might entertain the notion of going to see Frankie. I had imagined returning to Frankie's arms, perhaps as a part-time lover, as if I believed he would actually allow so little from me. My brain would not have been able to wrap around this...but my body isn't having the same difficulty. *I want him.*

As much as I ever wanted Frankie.

I want Pierre-Louis.

I want him to fuck me, but I also want to find out what naughtiness we can get ourselves into. My mind runs amok with images and ideas. What we could do together…

I see him topping me.

I see me equally topping him and honestly the second run of fantasies—him on his knees before me, licking my stilettos, me grabbing his short crop of hair and jerking his head back to make him look at me—is preferable.

His fingers find my clit, rolling over, teasing, drawing moans from my mouth. God, oh god.

Frankie said no role, no topping, no bottoming, but in my mind I am topping him. I am asking him to please Mistress. Where in the hell did that come from?

I smack his face and tell him he will have to try harder to please me…

"Ohgodohgodohgod."

Chapter Six

හ

In Chicago I am well used to driving past an array of varying-sized McMansions. Frankie's manor is a fine specimen of what a Chicago mansion looked like pre-cookie-cutter architecture. An obvious show of wealth doesn't astound me. Or at least it never did before riding through the French countryside where the homes of even the moderately well-off resemble castles. I gape...at the openness of the fields, at the sheer architectural beauty of the villages and châteaux, at the vineyards. Frankie's childhood home, Château de Hart, is no exception. I gape. Openly. The three-story brick manor is timeless and ancient, it is everything I expected and a hundred times more. The brick is a softly faded red, the shutters covering the windows freshly painted crisp white. It is both foreboding and inviting. Holy shit, he grew up here?

He points.

East. "Stables."

West. "Vineyards."

North. "Outdoor swimming pool, the gardens and *l'orangerie.*"

South. "Caretaker's house and chai."

He catches my gaze. "There are sixty-four acres, you have free roam of all of them. Try to not get lost and do not leave the grounds without an escort—either myself, Pierre-Louis or I have three trusted employees. Of course, you will ask permission should you require doing so."

I don't bat an eye even though I am shocked. I'd forgotten. So many restrictions, so little freedom. Can I really do this again? He smiles, motioning toward the house. "When you are ready, I'll show you around."

I try to take in the view of all that surrounds me. In the distance, ponies are romping in a field. I shade my eyes, scanning and easily finding where the vineyards begin. The sheer beauty of this country setting is too much. Too idyllic. As much as I dreamed…and more. I would very much like a closer look at the stables and I suppose at some point I will be given a tour of the chai. Part of the dream I had when we were together before was to help him with the day-to-day operations of the winery…

Regret for a lost past twists my heart. I reach out my hand to be pulled along inside. He announces rooms as we peek inside each on the ground floor. "Entrance hall, grand salon, dining hall, kitchen, office, library, interior courtyard."

It is too much magnificence. My entire Cape Cod would fit inside the interior courtyard. He points through the windows at the swimming pool, which is sparkling clean and well cared for. Just beyond the pool, the shining glass of the greenhouse, what he referred to as *l'orangerie*, is visible. He explains, "Nude sunbathing on nice days is expected." At my look of stark horror, he amends, "Unless we have guests."

"You have maids? Butlers?" I stammer.

He smiles. "My employees are well used to the way my household is run. They won't pay any attention whatsoever. The house rules are the same here as in Chicago. Both you and Pierre-Louis will be nude at all times unless we have visitors. Below us there are three wine cellars and of course the dungeon that has been converted to a rather entertaining playroom."

The dungeon, of course. I shiver, expecting that he is teasing me, betting he isn't. I sincerely hope he doesn't expect me to disrobe immediately.

"Ready to see the upper floors?" he asks.

I hate to be rude but I don't think I can take more tour in my five-inch heels. They are beautiful but painful. He starts toward the staircase. "Come, come."

I suck up the pain and follow him. Pierre-Louis requests permission to stay behind and make certain the kitchen is in good order for our stay. Frankie explains as we climb the stairs, "While we are here, Pierre-Louis will do much of the cooking and baking. It is what he enjoys. So, what is it you enjoy?"

I pause on the steps. What do I enjoy? It takes me a moment before I answer, "I still like to read."

"Ah, *oui*, my little bookworm. You will be happy to know the library is on the second floor."

Reaching the top step, he turns left and starts the tour. "There are thirteen bedrooms, seven on this floor, six on the floor above us. We will share this bedroom," he says as we enter a large suite. A wide window bank opens onto a balcony much like his bedroom in Chicago. He points to a second set of doors. "Through there is the bathroom. It will have a bedroom similar to this one on the other side. Pierre-Louis will stay there for now."

For now? Eyeing the supersized bed in the room, which was obviously built with three or more in mind, I don't ask. I turn to face him, letting out a small sigh. Stepping closer, he brushes his fingertips over my cheek before pulling me toward him for a kiss. Our mouths lock and I remember the hours we once spent just kissing. He steals my breath away, making me ache with want. Releasing me he asks, "You will let me share you with Pierre-Louis tonight?"

I understand it is not a question but a request. Still, I nod my assent, making him smile. He kisses me again and I find myself wishing we were here alone, no Pierre-Louis, but that dream was the one I walked away from. I had Frankie all to myself. Once. Threw it away. It seems my future, if it is to include Frankie, will also include Pierre-Louis.

You will let me share you with Pierre-Louis tonight? My mind is flying over the possibilities.

"You may disrobe now."

I pull from his grasp and walk over to the bed, where I sit on the upholstered bench at the foot to remove my shoes. I place the shoes on the floor before standing to shimmy from my jeans and pull my top over my head. I strip for him without self-consciousness. How many times have I stripped for this man? I start to remove my bra but he lifts a hand, signaling for me to wait. He motions for me to turn. I turn for him slowly, not once but twice, waiting for him to say "Stop." Isn't it funny how memories long forgotten return? This was one such moment. Turning for him, letting him see the handiwork of each mark he has left on my body. I am surprised when he says "Stop" after only two turns. He says, "Remove the rest."

I slide out of my bra and panties, then stand unmoving as he looks.

It is hard to stand under such scrutiny, so much easier when my body was in motion. With my body still, my mind is in motion, thinking too much about how he sees me. If he is disappointed by the extra pounds, the extra curves. He steps closer and his hand drops to the soft, girly curve of my belly. His fingers trace the deepest groove of my not so obvious stretch marks. I have four from my pregnancy, all faded to soft silvery-white lines, but one is dented and he found my imperfection immediately. I tighten my jaw, stiffen my spine. Did he expect me to be as beautiful as I was when I left, when I was twenty-six and at the height of my physical perfection?

He surprises me when he drops to one knee and kisses the scar. "I did not give you this mark."

"No," I whisper.

"I regret that, *ma belle*, because it is the most beautiful mark on your body."

When he stands and walks away, I am shocked, even more so when he exits the room, leaving me alone. He leaves me not knowing what to think, not knowing if or when he will come back. I don't follow him, though I wish to. Damn it, I'd forgotten how hard it is to be a silent, compliant, obedient sex slave…

I touch the dent low on my belly, remembering the flash of heat and itch one particular day late in my pregnancy. *The most beautiful mark.* Frankie obviously has regrets too. It pains me to believe he might have changed his mind about children had I stayed, that we might have formed a child together. I shake my head. Silly thoughts. "The past is what it is." There's no sense in regret and I love the daughters I did have and can't imagine life without them.

I am left looking around the lavishly decorated room. My bags have not only been delivered but unpacked, with all of my intimate clothing put away in drawers and my slacks, tops and dresses hung in the armoire. My shoes, jewelry and toiletries are also organized. Invisible servants. I look over my shoulder, expecting to see I am not alone after all. He said his staff was well trained. I'll say.

I open my purse and take out my cell phone, carrying it with me out onto the balcony. A brilliant sun falls over my nakedness, warming me. I sit on an upholstered chair and scroll through my phone, wanting to talk to my daughters. No, I need to talk to my daughters. A dose of reality is definitely in order, especially now that I am once again the very naked property of François de Hart.

"Mommy." Ellie answers, sounding much happier than the last time we spoke.

"Hi, beautiful." I sound high-pitched and nervous, probably because I am sitting out on a balcony—naked. Will I ever be able to get used to this again? I go back into the bedroom and rummage through a drawer until I find a comfortable shorts-and-shirt outfit to wear, dressing while we talk. The whole lounging around the house naked thing was fine when I was twenty-something, now it is uncomfortable, especially while talking to my daughters. "How's the boat?"

"Dreadful. We both got seasick and had to disembark." She giggles. "It was horrible, we were puking because of the motion sickness and then we started sympathy puking for each other. You should have seen it."

"Mm, the visual is enough, thanks," I assure her, laughing and thinking it must be genetics. "So what's the new plan? Did you see a doctor for some motion sickness pills?"

Her voice is full of disappointment when she says, "You didn't see my blog yet? We've joined up with a bus tour for a scenic drive through Italy. Then France. Then Spain. After that? Who knows."

"Oh, sweetheart," I say, feeling sympathetic, knowing a group bus tour is as far from an exciting Mediterranean cruise as night and day. I promise, "I'll look at your blog tonight, but that's actually why I called. Is your sister there beside you?"

"Of course. What's wrong?" Her voice switches from bored and desperate to concern in seconds. She sounds so much like her father…

I assure her nothing is wrong before asking her to put her cell on speaker. "I don't want you to worry, but I've decided to take a trip myself. I'm actually in France."

"You're planning on spying on us," Ells accuses.

"Oh, Mommy. Really? France? France isn't far at all." Bree exudes then yells to the others, "Mom's in France," and I assume she is making the announcement to my parents, knowing I've assumed correctly when I hear my mother in the background, "France? Your mother is in France?"

I interrupt them all, "I'm visiting friends and I have no intention of spying on you. Or interrupting your trip. I just wanted you to know I'm not in the States."

"You have friends in France?" Ells asks, sounding suspicious, and I decide she sounds exactly like her father.

"I do and it seemed like perfect timing to visit them."

"Let me have the phone," I hear my mother demand in the background.

"Charlotte?" Mother sounds concerned. "You're in France?"

"Yes." I laugh, trying to sound nonchalant. "I needed to get away and a friend invited me to France."

"The friend wouldn't be anyone I know? Would it?"

I've never been a very good liar, so I don't even try. "It's Frankie, Mom. I'm certain you'll remember."

"How could I forget the Frenchman?" she asks, making "the Frenchman" sound like "that asshole" without ever saying the word. I know that she thinks that he stole my heart and then broke it into a million pieces. I never corrected that assumption. Number one, I never wanted to talk about him again, never wanted to hear his name again, because I knew I would have lost my resolve and gone back to him. And number two, she never really liked him or approved of him too much. I think she thought he was too mysterious, but it was only that we kept most of our relationship a dark secret. I couldn't actually share that I was his sex slave, could I? She also thought he was too beautiful…for me.

"So, how is François?"

I sigh. This was not the conversation I'd intended on having. I lift my face into the baking sun, wishing I could just hang up and go find my Frenchman. I answer, "He's good. It was nice to hear from him again."

"He called you?"

"Yes. But does it matter? Who called whom?"

"It might," she answers furtively. "It just might."

I hear Frankie calling my name from outside and rush out to the balcony to look over the railing for him. He is standing on the far side of the yard between the pool and the greenhouse. He tilts his head, a questioning look on his face and I know it is because he just left me nude and now I am dressed again. He points to me and then toward the greenhouse. I smile, signaling I need a moment before pointing at the phone. He doesn't look impressed as he turns and walks toward the shining glass structure. I tell my mom, "I need to go. But call again soon, okay?"

Chapter Seven

ഗ

I hurry to the greenhouse, still wearing my shorts and shirt. I'm nervous because, technically, I was told to stay nude. Those are the house rules. Problem is, I don't know if I can abide by this rule and I don't know if it is negotiable, but I'm about to find out.

The smell of warm, damp earth and moss is my greeting. The greenhouse is hot and humid, the glass forming the walls drips with moisture. The heat seems a visible mist in the air. From behind me, Pierre-Louis sweeps me off my feet to hold me in his arms. I am surprised he is still wearing clothing. Obviously he was not yet instructed to disrobe. He carries me to the center of the room. Frankie is a step ahead, sweeping aside crockery and potting tools from the top of a wooden table. The surface is not clean, not by a long shot, but Pierre-Louis lays me down on top of the table.

My heart skips a beat when Frankie tosses a length of rope to Pierre-Louis and the man grabs my wrist to tie to the corner of the table, attaching the rope first to my wrist and then to the leg. While Pierre-Louis is tying my wrists, Frankie spreads my legs and starts tying my ankles. He asks, "How attached are you to the clothing you are wearing?"

It takes a second for the full weight of the question to become active thought. Obviously my outfit is at risk. I tell him, "Replaceable," even though I really adore the shorts.

"*Bon,*" he says. "Did I not say you and Pierre-Louis are to be nude at all times?"

I figure the question is rhetorical and so I don't answer. A second later, Pierre-Louis is blindfolding me, a moment more and there is a *snip, snip* sound near my ear, larger and heavier than scissors by the sound, possibly some type of pruning shears. I shiver, nervous, excited, strangely not scared being tied spread-eagle though I suppose if I dwelled too much I could make myself terrified.

Cool metal is rubbed against my cheek.

"Kiss it," Frankie commands, and in my head he feels very much like Master. Except for the first night when he caned me, I haven't really felt his dominance so much. The heavy metal presses down on my lips and I kiss it.

I decide grass clippers even though I can't see them, because the metal seemed flat against my mouth and if they were pruning shears they would feel curved. As they are drawn over my cheek, I can feel the solid edge and the sensation makes me shiver.

"Cut holes," Master instructs. "I want to see her breasts."

I feel a tug on my shirt, my nipple caught with fabric, making my heart jump into my throat before Pierre-Louis corrects and holds only fabric. I am relieved when I hear *snip, snip* but am not left in agonizing pain. When he releases the cloth I can feel my left nipple is sticking through the hole in my shirt and bra. He grabs the shirt over my right breast, tugging, not catching nipple. *Snip, snip.*

It feels odd having my nipples exposed. Frankie leans forward and takes my nipple into his mouth, though I am not one hundred percent certain it is Frankie and not Pierre-Louis until he makes a content sound in his throat. He sucks and bites, bringing my nipple to a tight, aroused point. He repeats on the other side. When he pulls his lips away I am left with a flash of pain in my right nipple and then immediately my left. I whimper from the pain. Nipple clamps. He tugs both and I realize the clamps are attached to a chain, which is confirmed when he puts the chain between my teeth with the command, "Bite."

I bite down, holding the chain.

Frankie says, "*Exposer sa chatte.*"

My brain translates effortlessly though it has been years and so I am not startled when I hear the snipping sound before I feel the metal hovering over my pussy. Pierre-Louis takes his time cutting a hole in my shorts, effectively making both the shorts and panties beneath crotchless, and I am glad he took his time.

The room is silent and still. I could almost believe the men disappeared into thin air for the quietness. There is a rustle above me and I hear a chirp. A bird is either in the greenhouse with us or landed on the roof. *Chir-wee, chir-wee.* I shiver, hoping the bird isn't in the building. It is silly perhaps in light of my being tied, my clothing cut, but the thought of a bird landing anywhere near me, worse, on me, creeps me out.

Chir-wee, chir-wee.

"Pull the chain, Cassiopeia."

I tug the chain caught between my teeth, stretching out my nipples, sending fresh waves of pain through them after having forgotten the clamps were even attached.

"Jerk the clamps off."

Me? Oh shit.

I pull but it is not nearly hard enough. It hurts. I pull harder and the clamp on my left breast pops off, my back arching as the pain shoots from tit to spine. "Goddamn." I cry out, wishing I wasn't tied so I could fold into myself, fold into the pain. The chain drops from my mouth.

Master says, "Tsk, tsk. Now how will you get the other clamp off?"

I shrug, tossing my head.

"You may ask my assistant."

I ask softly, "Pierre-Louis, will you take the nipple clamp off?"

He asks Master, "Sir, may I remove the clamp for Cassiopeia?"

"No," he answers tersely. "She must do it herself."

I am glad I have the blindfold over my eyes so that he doesn't see me roll my eyes. "Pierre-Louis, will you put the chain back in my mouth?"

He asks, "Sir, may I help Cassiopeia by putting the chain back into her mouth?"

"*Oui.*"

I hear a rustle in the foliage between me and the windows. I tense, guessing the bird is in the room even before I hear the chirp. *Chir-wee, chir-wee.* I shiver. Pierre-Louis puts the cool metal chain back in my mouth and I pull as hard as I can, popping the clamp off and screaming when it seems to hurt twice as much as the first did. I feel a warm, wet mouth closing over the screaming flesh and I am not sure whose mouth it is. It feels so good after the pain, my body throbs with the pleasure of the soft suckle. My hips move on the tabletop, my pussy clenching, wanting attention. I can feel myself growing wetter by the second, the cool drip of my fluid sliding between my ass cheeks.

There is a sound next to me on the table, a rustling I imagine is the bird. I listen more closely, tensing, relaxing after heart-pounding minutes, probable only seconds, realizing it is not the bird, it is either Master or Pierre-Louis doing something, perhaps laying out floggers or other sundry items. I understand the sound very quickly as having been the soft rattle of wooden clothing pins when Master tells Pierre-Louis, "The sensitive skin inside her upper arms, the inside of her thighs," and Pierre-Louis very quickly and efficiently starts attaching the pinch-type wooden pins. My pussy clenches with each attachment, pinch, pinch, pinch, just under my right armpit where the skin is supersensitive on both arms, then again under my left arm. Pinch. Pinch. Pinch. I feel his warm hands between my thighs, pushing up the legs of my shorts to get them where he wants them. Pinch, pinch, pinch. He moves left to right. Pinch, pinch, pinch.

When he finishes the room is silent again. They are waiting, watching. Then suddenly, I feel warm fingers smooth over my labia. Master says softly, "I think two more."

I know he is attaching the last two, pulling my labia lips apart to attach one left, one right. It hurts. I bounce my knees a little but I don't cry out. He says, "Good girl," and it makes me feel all warm and fuzzy inside. How I went two decades without such affirmations is beyond me now that I am here with him again.

"Remove the shirt."

The steel of the grass trimmers slides up my side as Pierre-Louis cuts away the remaining fabric. He pulls the shirt away, jerking it from under my back. He knocks off one of the clothes clips and the pain is intense.

Master says, "Leave it," and I assume he means to not reattach it. He lifts the blindfold from my eyes and his gaze is questioning but I don't understand what he is asking. He pulls his gaze from me to look at Pierre-Louis. "I want to watch her suck you."

"Sir?"

"Strip. Now. Straddle her face."

No one asks me how I feel about it. I am merely the object to be shared between two men. It is a perverse delight that I am excited by the prospect. I have seen Pierre-Louis completely nude and he is an amazing attribute to the male species. We have kissed and he has touched me intimately, but I have not touched him. I try not to watch as he unbuttons his shirt but flexing, bunched abdominals are hard to look away from. He slides out of his shirt and tosses it aside. He unbuttons the top button of his jeans, unzips, stops to take a wrapped condom out of a front pocket, then strips the rest of the way.

Unrolling the condom down his length he says lightly, "Strawberry. I hope you like that flavor."

I actually detest flavored condoms, but then I hate any condom. I know Frankie know this and yet...

I can't debate the reasons as my mind is shocked by the sudden shift of weight. The wooden table groans a little as he climbs on to it and moves into position, one leg warm against my ribs. But he needs to be closer, and when he shoves his knee under my armpit another clip flies free. *Oh.*

Master reaches to remove the remaining four pins and my body jerks with the removal of each. Then he steps away, standing where I can't see him. I wonder what he is thinking, what he was asking me but didn't say. I don't have time to dwell on that though because Pierre-Louis swings his leg over my chest and his weight is straddling me, though not his entire weight. Very little of it in fact, merely enough to let me know he is there, in position, knees high under my arms. His erect penis bobs in front of my face. His gaze locks on mine but I don't change my focus, I look intently at his eyes.

He strokes my jaw, angles my face and draws his thumb lightly over my bottom lip. He smells earthy and warm, a hint of spicy cologne mingled with the scent of clean man. The tip of his erection closely follows. I open my mouth and he slides in, not deep, just a little. Strawberries and rubber. *Lovely.* I focus on what I am supposed to be doing and not the horrid taste in my mouth. I stroke circles with my tongue around the glans before latching on for some fast hard sucks. He presses deeper even though I could suck and play with the head of his cock all day. He slides it all the way in so that he bumps the back of my throat, leaving me fighting the gag reflex. He backs it out enough for me to relax and suck but almost immediately pushes back in. "I want you to swallow his dick, Cassiopeia. Show him you know what to do with a man's cock." I hear Master whispering close to my face, his breath warm on my cheek. I jerk my head, looking, realizing only then how close he is, how close he has been all this time. He is squatted behind the table, seeing Pierre-Louis from almost the same angle that I see him.

"Yes, Master," I say around Pierre-Louis's hard flesh in my mouth. He pushes deeper and I try, but we are at the wrong angle. Swallowing him seems impossible, tied as I am. He pushes farther, gagging me. I sputter. I'm not sure which is more arousing for me, the fact I am making him moan or the sound I make gagging around his cock. All I know is that I want him to fuck me. My hips rock and my pussy clenches around nothing, the weight of the clothespins heavy on my labia.

"Keep sucking," he commands, standing, walking away. "Don't even think about stopping."

Sucking I can do. Pierre-Louis pulls out just enough for me to hold him solidly in my mouth, rolling my tongue over him and sucking without any gagging.

I feel Master at my ankles, his touch light as he slides up my legs. He releases each of the clips on my inner thighs. "Ow. Owwwww."

My hips buck but I keep sucking.

He removes one of the clips from my labia and I scream, trying to roll away from the pain, my ankles pulling against the rope. I keep Pierre-Louis' cock in my mouth, moaning around it. I feel Master's finger rub along the screaming flesh, helping the blood flow to return quicker and it hurts and feels good equally. I try to push harder against his caressing fingers. He releases the second clothespin. "Holy fuck."

He smacks my labia as if he is spanking them, and I am close enough to orgasm I think I might. "Ohgodohgodohgod," I say, or try to say.

"Tell me what you need, Cassiopeia."

Pierre-Louis thrusts in and out of my mouth as I curse and beg, making anything I am saying fairly unintelligible. "I want you to fuck me, Master," becomes "I-on-ew-ew-uuu-eee-aa-er."

The table groans and I realize Master's weight has been added. He lifts my hips and fills me in a long, deep stroke.

I close my eyes, blocking the image of Pierre-Louis's face as Master rubs his finger over my clit and thrusts, matching the rhythm of Pierre-Louis thrusting in and out of my mouth.

Pierre-Louis tenses, going still and I know he is coming, filling the condom. He pulls his spent length from my mouth and Master keeps thrusting and rubbing. Pierre-Louis tweaks my nipple, pinching, pulling. Helping? Distracting? God, oh god. I am so close to orgasm. I moan and toss my head.

Pierre-Louis shoves two fingers in my mouth and I suck, bucking against Master's touch, feeling him deep inside me, thrusting, thrusting.

Sucking.

Thrusting.

We both moan, his moan heightening my need, whisking me higher, and then I am plummeting, my orgasm jerking through my body, lighting every nerve with fire.

* * * * *

I am still bound and lying on top of the dirty wood potting table. The men talk in low voices from somewhere inside the greenhouse, though I guess it could just as easily be outside the main doors because their voices are soft and indiscernible, leaving me too much time to fixate on doubts. The sex was amazing, always has been, but there is something missing that was there before but is gone now. Is it me? Is it the way I feel, being twenty years older, not so blindly obsessed?

At approaching footsteps I turn my head and see Master. He kisses me. Gently. Tenderly. "*Merci, ma belle.*"

I smile against his lips as he kisses me again. "*Merci?*"

"For returning to me… But it seems to me you do not have your heart in it."

My heart stills in my chest then jumps before returning to its pace, faster than before.

"I have sent Pierre-Louis to the kitchen to start preparing dinner so I may have you to myself for a while. I hope you don't mind."

I shake my head. Mind? How could I mind when his touch on my face speeds my heart, his words both terrifying and comforting me at the same time.

"You put your clothing back on. Did you even wait for me to be down the hall?" The sting of his words is softened by his gentle hands rubbing over my breasts.

I shake my head.

He pinches a nipple softly, pulling ever so slightly, but they are still sensitive from the clothespins and so I suck in my breath. "Do you wish to explain yourself?"

I rush to do just that. "I was talking to my daughters on the—"

"Shh." He silences me. "I did not say 'explain,' I said 'do you wish to offer an excuse?'"

Ah. Still a stickler for details. "Master, I do wish to explain."

"*Oui*, I am certain you do." He rubs his hand over my stomach. "However, do you remember my policy on excuses?"

Our gazes lock. Of course I remember. How could I not remember?

"Should you be punished, Cassiopeia?"

I whisper softly. "Yes, Master."

"*Oui*," he says, kissing me gently again. I lift my face, basking in the sweetness of his lips, knowing this bliss will soon be replaced with torment. He strokes my face. "I think instead of punishing you, I would prefer to play with you a bit more. Would that be acceptable?"

I sob with relief. "Yes."

Playing with Frankie is always extreme—before, with Pierre-Louis, it was as though we were still getting to know each other—now, he won't hold back. "Yes, Master."

He unties my wrists and ankles then helps me to sit up. I cross my legs, sitting still in the center of the table. I rub my wrists, not because the ropes were tied too tight but because of the phantom rope making me feel still tied. Touching my skin helps me realize I am free. He is as nude as I. He runs his hand over my shoulder, asking, "What would you like me to do to you?"

My eyebrow arches. I ask, "I'm being given a choice?"

"*Oui*, of course."

Oui, of course? Okay, where is the alien mother ship? The Master of old didn't do things this way. "I like when you bind me. I like it when you hurt me."

He winks at me, his eyes filling with mischief. "*Oui*, but tell me how you want me to tie you, tell me how you want me to hurt you."

My brain trips over itself and then it jumps to the memory always called to my thoughts when I was lying bored under John, waiting for him to come. Sometimes, I even got excited enough to join him with an orgasm of my own. I readjust on the tabletop so I am squatting in front of him. "Do you remember when you used to attach a spreader bar between my ankles and hobble my thighs to my calves?"

He smiles wickedly and rubs his chin. "You always cursed me when I did that to you. Now you tell me you liked it?"

"I hated it."

He looks at me with new interest. He rubs his hands over my thighs and I tremble beneath his touch. "But first I should tie your hands."

"Behind my back?"

"I think to your ankles for what I have in mind."

I swallow hard, my mouth going dry.

"How would I hurt you, Cassiopeia?"

"Maybe you could use your imagination."

He laughs loudly and I think how rarely it has been that I have ever heard him laugh. Has Pierre-Louis brought about this change in him? "I like to hear you laugh."

His lips twitch. "I like to hear you scream. Let's see what we can do about making us both happy, eh?"

A rope I did not realize he was holding whizzes around my ankle. He cinches it tight before wrapping it around my thigh and tightening it in a loop at my ankle. He repeats the action with my other leg. I am already trembling and can't imagine staying in this squat much longer, but we are just beginning.

"Spreader bar?" he asks.

I nod and he looks around the room, settling on a broom. He shrugs almost apologetically before tying my ankles and wrists to the handle. "Feel steady?"

"Yes, Master." Surprisingly. It's been a long time, I'm surprised I'm still limber enough to do this at all. Thank god for yoga DVDs.

"Comfortable?"

"For now."

He stands looking at me and purses his lips. "You didn't like the clothespins on your pussy lips, did you?" It must be a rhetorical question because he reaches forward to pinch my exposed labia. "Very tender? A little tender?"

"A little," I answer softly.

He opens a drawer built into the tabletop and pulls out a ball of twine. He picks up two wooden clothespins and wraps the ends. I think I hear him humming under his breath but all I can think about is my shaking knees and the dread filling the pit of my stomach, knowing he is going to attach the clamps to my labia again. I seriously used to fantasize about this? Really?

He stretches out the skin of my labia, clamping on the first clothespin solidly. I squeal.

He smiles and it is beautiful. "Does it hurt?"

"Yes, goddammit."

He stretches the twine, stretching out my labia lip, pulling, hurting me. I stare at the clothespin lying on the table, waiting, but he doesn't make me wait long. He attaches it to the other side. I whine to keep my voice silent, to keep from screaming and cursing. Tears slide over my cheeks and he looks at my face with a surprised expression. He collects one of my tears on his fingertip and traces it to its source. "It hurts this bad?"

I shake my head. I fantasized about this because I needed this.

His forehead furrows as he studies my face.

"I'm okay," I assure him.

The tears are pure emotion, not from pain. When my grandmother had a stroke a few years ago and I volunteered to take her to physical therapy, the therapist explained that when she cried, claiming she couldn't do the exercises because it hurt, it was her tears that told him she was in emotional pain. Yes, she was upset because she was disabled and struggling with simple tasks. If it was true pain, the therapist explained, she would be moaning, or screaming. No one understood it, not my mother or my mother's sisters, they wanted a different therapist, thinking the one she had was a sadist. I believed the therapist because I understood a bit about the workings of pain. I think Master understands as well, because he takes my face between his hands and kisses away the tears, drawing the salty moisture to my lips when he kisses me. He whispers against my mouth, "I have missed you," and I whisper back, "I missed you."

My knees are shaking, my ankles screaming, and my toes feel as if they are on fire, but none of that matters while he kisses me. He is the center of my universe and I am the center of his.

"Talk to me, Cassiopeia. Tell me what has happened since last night and today."

"Twenty years." My answer is pithy.

He looks disappointed and then he is suddenly releasing me. "I had hoped you were true to your word, that you loved me, that you were returning to me fully, but it seems I am a fool."

He walks away, keeping his back to me.

I collapse onto the table, my legs refusing to support me another second, or that could be what I wished it was. Truly, I was defeated. I knew I was ruining everything.

Yes, I'm confused how I will ever be a sex slave and a mother.

Yes, I'm confused as to where I fit into Master and Pierre-Louis's life.

I don't want to throw it away. Not yet. Not without a fight.

"I'll arrange for your transportation back to the United States."

"Please, don't. It's hard talking to you."

He turns around but doesn't say anything.

"Before, when I was here, I was so much younger. There was little talking. Just orders, obeying, and now everything is different."

"Would you prefer we never talk? That I allow you to wallow in your thoughts and needs and desires without allowing you to express them? Because that worked so well before."

I close my eyes and try to harness my thoughts. "I like the way you are now more. I want to be able to talk to you, share my thoughts and feelings and ideas with you."

Opening my eyes, I meet his gaze and hold out my hand to him. I'm very glad when he steps forward and takes it. "I'm afraid. I don't know where I fit in. You and Pierre-Louis have such a strong, committed relationship, and we no longer do."

"It will take time to rebuild what we once had."

"I know."

"And the dynamics of a ménage are complicated and complex, but we will work things out."

"You sound so confident."

He leans forward and kisses me. His lips linger over mine as he asks, "You love me?"

"Yes, desperately. I can't imagine going back to my old life."

"After only a few days, you feel this way?"

I nod my head rapidly.

"That is why I am confident." His lips brush mine.

"I have so many doubts."

"Set them free."

"Easier said than done."

"Because Pierre-Louis is younger? Is that your doubt? Because John cheated on you and devalued your worth, you feel inferior?"

I swallow hard, not liking the truth so much.

"It will not matter how much I tell you that you are beautiful. It will not matter how much Pierre-Louis tells you that you are beautiful. You have to see it for yourself. You have to find in yourself what we see that transcends physical beauty."

He's right. I know he's right. I press my forehead to his.

"What do you want from me, Cassiopeia? What do you need?"

I kiss his cheek. "Make love to me."

He pushes me down onto the table. "Make love to you. Worship you."

I don't understand until he takes my hand and starts kissing the length from fingertips to shoulder. "This arm is the most beautiful arm in the world, and I am a blessed man every time it wraps around me."

The trail of kisses continues, over my shoulder and up my neck. "The most beautiful shoulder, the most beautiful neck —"

I giggle. "Okay, okay."

He kisses my eyelids. "The most beautiful eyes because they reflect your pleasure, your pain, your need, your desire. Flames fill your eyes when you look at me and I swear I will be burned alive by your passion. You make me a better man because I don't ever want to disappoint you. I have to meet your passion and help you take it even higher."

My pussy grows wet and needy. *Enough talking.* My hips come off the table, but he presses my pelvis down with his palm. "Not yet. I'm not through worshiping you. I haven't even gotten so far as your breasts."

"I could die of old age before you ever get to my clit."

"You're such a funny girl," he says but his mouth closes over mine and I am glad that he's finally quiet. I don't know if I'll ever get used to this new, improved Master, so in touch with his emotions and feelings that he wants to share them.

His mouth drops to my breast and he takes my nipple into his mouth and suckles. "You have the most beautiful breasts and now these glorious nipples have known the joys of nursing an infant…"

How does he know that? My guess is Paulette.

"My only regret is not sharing bringing a life into the world with you. Watching you nurse our child."

Oh God. Stop this. Don't say anything else.

Thankfully his lips drop to my stomach but my gratitude comes too soon. "Watching your stomach expand from afar, knowing another man's child grew in your womb. It changed me, Cassiopeia, because I knew I'd made a terrible mistake, one I would pay for with a lifetime away from you. I vowed then, if I could ever have another chance, I would give you anything you wanted."

Tears slide down my face, but I'm not alone. I feel Master's tears fall on my thighs as he begins his erotic litany about my beautiful legs. My toes. And finally, thankfully, my clit. His tongue is like wet flames and he is an erotic demon.

I'd forgotten how well he did *this*.

"Holy mother of God."

"So soon?"

I buck as he flicks and licks.

"Yes!"

A finger slides inside me and then a second. I am shaking and spasming around him. "Master! Master!"

"*Oui*, Cassiopeia. I am your Master."

Chapter Eight

ᔆᴐ

And then I sleep alone.

I'm not sure what I expected...the world to revolve around me, maybe.

I have to assume the hours spent in the greenhouse before dinner in a tender embrace, rebuilding some of what we lost, were meant to be a balm to my soul as I lie alone in the dark. I am not the sun, I am merely one of two moons that revolve around Frankie.

It is a warm night and I have the double doors to the balcony open to allow in the breeze and the night sounds — insects, bats, small nocturnal animals. After worrying so much about a bird when I couldn't see, now I want the distraction from any other noises that might waft through the house. I haven't heard anything. No conversation, no moans, no whistled strikes or flogged thuds. I'm a pervert. I don't want to hear it but I am disappointed when I hear nothing.

I could be nosy.

I could amble down the hallway toward the kitchen. I am a bit parched, perhaps to get a glass of water...and perchance to hear. Something.

Do I really, honestly want to hear them making love?

God. I hate this.

Frankie loves Pierre-Louis. Pierre-Louis loves Frankie. *Je t'aime. Je t'aime. Je t'aime.* Their mornings begin with the greeting, their conversations end with the words, and throughout the day, "*Je t'aime,*" for no reason.

I know, I know. Pierre-Louis could have the same complaint. Why am I jealous of one night? It's one night. And

I'm too sore and too exhausted to be included anyway. Too grumpy as well.

I want to throw something and break it for no good reason and I am not a temper tantrum kind of girl. I never was before.

I fling back the covers and climb out of bed, pacing, wondering what I could throw that would make me feel better but wouldn't get noticed by the cleaning staff or worse, Frankie.

Nothing.

I got nothing but an angry beast trying to climb out of my body.

I am in the hallway and standing in front of Pierre-Louis' bedroom door before I even realize I am out of my bed. My chest is heaving with emotion, my breath heavy, and I force myself to calm down. I want to go home. I want my life back. I want simple back.

I raise my fist but don't pound on the door.

I hear Frankie's voice. "Do you like that?"

I close my eyes and drop my fist to my side.

"Ahhh-ha-ha, yes-s-s," he hisses.

"And this?"

He moans, "Oh god, Master, what you do to me."

I walk backward from the door, colliding softly with the hall wall. My imagination spins wildly out of control as I listen, though I am not sure whether this is helping or hurting my jealous heart. With a shaky breath I go back to my room. I would not deny Pierre-Louis his pleasure just as he did not deny mine earlier today. If nothing else, we can all be civil about this, right?

I don't want to go home. Not really. What is there besides loneliness? And tonight I am feeling a lot of things, but lonely isn't one of them.

Morning comes too early since I fell asleep only the hour before dawn, the birds beginning to salute the day with their song. I am startled awake by one of Frankie's servants. It is rare to see them, and I have never been woken by one of them. She knocks softly before entering. "*Madame?*"

I sit up in the bed, startled.

"Monsieur requests you join him in the vineyard immediately."

I frown, nodding I understand the message though I'm confused as to why he didn't knock on the door himself. I don't dress, I throw on my long silk robe, yellow printed with a bright floral pattern. I clip my hair up and grab the cup of coffee the maid left on my nightstand for me on the way out the door and swallow half of it before I get down the stairs, the rest before I step out into the bright sun, leaving the empty cup on a low table in the foyer. I regret not putting on shoes as I cross the dew-damp grass, my bare toes cold and covered in grass clippings. It is only when I am within the rows of vines that I remember the robe and that I shouldn't be wearing it. *Twenty years of habit will be hard to break.* When I see Frankie and realize he sees me coming, I know it is too late to do anything about it.

He is walking between his grapes and I hurry to join him.

"I saw the dew still clinging to the fruit and wanted you to see," he tells me, looking at the cluster of grapes he is holding and not me. His tone and mood seem somber. I bite my lip, wondering if my worries were well founded last night. I walk beside him, distressed he will send me away because he loves Pierre-Louis so dearly.

"I used to dream of being here, with you," I say nervously, reaching out a finger to touch the cluster of small damp grapes. Water droplets drip off with the contact. "I made a dream journal and filled it with pictures of France and vineyards and you."

"*Oui*, I know." He turns his back and walks between the rows, seeming to inspect the vines as he does so.

I quickly follow. "It is different than I thought it would be."

"Because of Pierre-Louis?"

I shrug.

"You wish for me to send him away?"

"What?" I gasp, wondering if he would, if I asked. "No. I—" I stop walking. "He loves you, you love him."

He stops walking too and turns to face me, looking at me for the first time since I joined him. He looks as though he hasn't slept. I wonder if I look as bad. "Has Pierre-Louis asked you to get rid of me?"

He cocks his head sideways and takes a step forward. When he reaches to touch my shoulder, I feel his hand tremble. Oh. This is bad.

"*Au contraire.*"

Our gazes collide.

"He wants to spend time alone with you, giving the two of you time to get to know one another outside of the dynamic."

"The dynamic?" I ask.

"Me," he says, explaining, "He wants to see what will happen when you are both alone and not obeying my whims."

I shiver, thinking no good will come of this. I laugh, "Of course you said no."

He holds my chin so that I can't pull away from his gaze when he asks, "Is that what you wish?"

I force myself to stay very still beneath his hand. I refuse to admit I've seen the way Pierre-Louis looks at me with desire. Or that I want to be the one to wipe the arrogant look off his mouth by topping him, by making him beg. There is no good answer to this question because to deny I want the same thing would only plant the seeds of relationship destruction. I am too curious about the man in Frankie's bed. Too jealous. "I don't know what to think."

He takes my hands and leads me through the rows of healthy vines, their leaves green, their branches covered with clusters of still young grapes. "Don't think, tell me what you want."

"Are you asking if I want to fuck Pierre-Louis for the mere sake of fucking? The answer is no. In my mind Pierre-Louis is yours, just as I am yours."

"You think he is beautiful to gaze upon."

He says it as a statement not a question. Does that mean he's noticed I like to look at the man? Hell, who wouldn't? I squeeze his hand but have nothing to say.

"I risk losing the two of you to each other if I do nothing."

"What?" I gasp. "That's absurd."

"Is it? When I see how the two of you look at each other? I wanted to share you —" He leans closer and I think he will kiss me, but he only arches his brow. "I want the three of us to fit well together, but in order for that to work, the two of you must fit well together. Not so well you no longer have room for me though, so I think I need you and him to spend some time together."

I back away, shaking my head. "I've only just returned to you. I want you — not him."

"It is okay for you to want us both. You desire him."

"No," I deny, but it isn't the truth and we both know that. "I'm curious about him only. I wonder what it is about him that you love him so."

He pulls me close, wraps an arm around my waist and grips my hair in his other hand so that he can jerk my head back. He kisses me senseless. Damn. I feel as though I passed a test. Was he insecure I would want Pierre-Louis instead of him? I wrap my arms around his waist, pulling him closer. His erection presses solidly into my thigh. When he releases me, he says, "After we tour the vines, I want you to shower and get dressed. Pierre-Louis is going to show you around the countryside the next few days."

I gasp. "What?"

He tucks my hair behind my ear. "A small holiday for the two of you to get to know each other the way I know each of you."

I try to pull away but he holds me tight around the waist. I argue, "This is insane. Absurd. I already told you —"

He silences me with two fingers pressed to my lips. "I will hear no more. You will go on a holiday with Pierre-Louis to get to know who he is. That is all."

My eyes narrow. I'm not certain I understand. "Could you clarify what is expected?"

He shrugs. "I have no expectations. Pierre-Louis will have no expectations."

"And if he tries to," I look down at my wet toes, heart fluttering, mind galloping away on a wild stallion of lust, considering all of the possibilities, "seduce me?"

He chuckles, lifting my chin. "I have no doubt. Give yourself permission to enjoy his seduction. He is very good at giving pleasure. He is very romantic, a lover of life. I will not command you to have sex with him, nor will I forbid it. I only assume the natural course of events."

He kisses me before taking my hand to complete our tour of the vines.

So, what? Master has spoken? Obey without question? "I don't want to do this."

"It is not a choice."

"If I refuse to go?"

"The staff will pack your things."

I'll be forced to leave. I knew as much but I had to hear the words. There is no room for democracy in our relationship. I fight back tears. I do not want to be seduced by Pierre-Louis.

I do not want my suspicions confirmed that my heart is fickle. No, not my heart. Never my heart. Just my pussy.

"What do you fear, Charlotte?"

Charlotte? Not even Cassiopeia? I can't stop the sob. "I don't want to lose you. Again."

"Then you obey. Without question. Simple."

"Yes, Master." My eyes drop to the ground.

"And Charlotte?"

Charlotte. Still? "Yes, Master?" I don't look up.

"You will burn the robe on your return to the house."

I gasp. *But this is my favorite robe. Briana and Ellie gave it to me for Mother's Day several years ago.* A tear slides down my cheek. "Yes, Master."

I turn and run from him, not caring that twigs and stones are jabbing my feet. My heart is breaking over what I must do but it is my own damn fault. *Why do I keep breaking the simplest rules?*

I am out of breath when I exit the vineyards but still run across the lawn toward the house. The scent of smoke leads me to a trash-burning barrel behind the kitchen. A man I don't recognize is turning the contents with a pitchfork.

I strip and hold the silk robe against my cheek. I can't believe I'm doing this. I could leave. I could go home and get on with my life. Forget Frankie forever. Wait for my daughters to come home from their summer adventure.

I could just go back to being Charlotte.

Damn it.

With tears blurring my sight, I wad the fabric up and drop it into the barrel. I can't watch it burn so I turn away quickly.

I am startled by the touch on my shoulder. Even more surprised when I turn to find the servant holding my robe out to me from the end of his pitchfork. He nods toward the vineyard and I see Frankie poised at its edge. *Don't disobey me again.*

He doesn't say the words, but I hear them just the same. I don't understand his change of heart, or how he signaled the servant to prevent the robe from burning. The Master of old would have watched it go up in flames. I do not know this man watching me from across the yard.

I snatch the robe, thankful despite my questions, and hurry to my room. Inspection of the fabric reveals two small singed holes, but the damage only makes the robe dearer to my heart as I hold the sunshine-hued silk to my face and sob. I can't escape the mental image of my daughters' brilliant smiles when I opened their present and exclaimed with delight. How could I ever have faced them again without guilt?

* * * * *

Standing, waiting in the driveway of the château, I am packed and ready to go on holiday with Frankie's lover. The men are both still inside, leaving me waiting outside for twenty minutes. I seem too anxious. I wish it was because I believe the earlier we get started the sooner the task will be completed, as if it was some horrible chore, but the truth is my heart has been skipping around my chest with giddy abandon, which is absurd. I love Frankie. I don't need a second lover. But God, he's glorious to look upon. I've never been so affected by lust.

I'm an intelligent woman. I can see there are clearly two paths. Utopia, where the three of us learn to live and love each other completely. Ruination, where one or all of us are destroyed by each other's jealousy.

How did my life take such a strange turn?

I could have said no to all of it, beginning the night I received the bustier, but the honest truth is I feel so alive when I am with Frankie—before my children, and now since the reunion. All between seems like a cushioned dream with little vibrancy or vitality.

I let out a deep sigh when the chauffeur drives the car up to the doors. This is really happening.

Behind me, I hear both men step on to the stoop to join me in the bright sunshine of midday. Only one joins me in the backseat of the car. I turn to look at Pierre-Louis, thinking that any moment the bubble will break and I will come to my senses and explain that I can't go, but when I catch his gaze he smiles softly, and I know this moment was destined from the day we first laid eyes on the other.

"I am glad you agreed to this holiday." He touches my hand and an electric wave seems to zip up my arm.

The car drives away from the château and I realize I didn't wave at Frankie. I turn and wave through the rear window. He returns the gesture but I still feel like an idiot. I turn back around and face front, not looking at Pierre-Louis. He reaches over and takes my hand. I don't pull away from his touch but I can't meet his gaze. I look at the leather seat in front of me, not even paying attention to the changing view until I lose track of time and am surprised when the vehicle comes to a stop. The view from my window isn't reassuring — rows and rows of bicycles and pedestrians milling around wearing the same bright yellow shirts. Pierre-Louis squeezes the hand I'd forgotten he was holding. "I hope you can ride."

"You're serious?"

His answer is a beaming smile as our chauffeur opens my door and steps to the side so I might exit. "I'm not sure about this," I say, mostly to no one in particular. Pierre-Louis readily assures me with a soft whisper close to my ear. "Trust us."

Us? Did he mean trust me? Or did he actually mean us? And by us did he mean Frankie? Of course, who else would he mean? But why a bike tour?

Thirty minutes later I am matched with a bicycle, wearing a bright yellow tour company-logo-imprinted shirt and an equally ugly helmet. I am geared up with bicycle gear I never knew existed, including special shoes anatomically curved for more efficient pedaling. Pierre-Louis dons a pair of sporty sunglasses that mold around his eyes and I am about to comment that he looks as if he's done this before, thinking he looks incredibly hot, when he hands me a pair of similar shades.

Accepting them, I thank him and ask, "Do I look as dorky as I feel?"

He winks. "You are a goddess."

I snort and mount the bicycle, glad I've managed to stay in somewhat athletic condition by keeping up with my daughters. I hope it is enough as we take off in a pack. There are twenty-two of us as we pedal down the drive headed to god knows where, but the sun is shining and I feel strangely good. I feel as if I should be feeling irritation or out of my element or horribly manipulated, but I don't. This is a sudden, unexpected turn of events. Much better than riding side by side, tense and uneasy about what is going to happen next.

Our tour guide explains as we ride. The Boudreaux bike trip begins in a region called Entre Deux Mers. "This is the Bordeaux's least heralded region, but I believe, as I feel you will soon agree, its most beautiful area. As we spread out, feel free to stop and take photographs at your leisure. Do not worry if the group gets ahead of you because we will all end at the Château de Sade. If you look to your left, we are passing now a kiwi grove."

The name of the château is probably a gimmick, I decide, looking over the other guests. Though they are in reasonably good shape, mostly men, I just don't get a high-kink vibe. An hour into this adventure I think I am probably in over my head as the rolling hills feel like mountains to my calves and thighs. Only a true masochist could enjoy this torture. I look at Pierre-Louis, he isn't struggling. Did I expect him to be? He is twenty-eight and obviously in very fit condition.

I am ready to call it quits as we head into our second hour, but the road evens out and I find we are winding through a dense, ancient forest. It is peaceful and perfect and appears to be ripped from the pages of a fairy tale, as the pointed tower of a castle appears from nowhere. We don't stop as a dozen others do to take photos. Pierre-Louis takes the lead as I trail behind and I begin to worry I am holding him back.

The forest breaks into an open field. Yellow flowers on either side of the road mock the bright shirts on our backs. I see Pierre-Louis has pulled off to the side of the road, waiting for my slow ass to catch up, no doubt. He dismounts and puts down his kickstand. We're stopping? I could jump for joy as I pull up beside him and dismount as well. Too tired for jumping, my legs tremble and I am embarrassed I am so out of shape. If he notices, he doesn't mention it. I watch him throw back his head to guzzle water from his sports bottle and decide to do the same. I am swallowing when he says, "I would love to lay you down in that field of mustard and make love to you."

I choke and sputter on the water. He thumps my back, apologizing and laughing.

"You took me by surprise."

He looks at me and I realize how serious he is. My mouth opens and shuts but no words come out. I focus on the brilliant, cheery yellow flowers, not committing to a negative or positive response. He takes my hand and kisses my knuckles, promising, "Soon."

I meet his gaze, wondering if the lust in my eyes matches the intensity in his.

Chapter Nine

🔊

Sighting the château, I could weep, knowing a hot bath and gourmet meal await me. I wonder if they would deliver the meal to me in my bath…

Seeing Pierre-Louis decked out in silk shirt, tie and suit coat, any thought of bowing out of going to dinner with him leaves my head. I am wrapped in a towel, hair dried and styled, makeup on, but still not dressed. He whistles softly. "If you are this enchanting in a towel, I am truly in trouble once you put on the dress François sent over for tonight."

Frankie sent a dress? I shiver, letting my gaze follow Pierre-Louis' glance to the bed. Oh God. He really sent over a dress and he obviously meant for me to look and feel sexy in it. I walk over to inspect it, picking it up by its hanger, holding it at arm's reach as if it is the snake from the Garden of Eden. It is an above-the-knee-length, strapless chiffon dress in the softest shade of cream, beaded over the top. It is sinfully luxurious. "Doesn't this make you feel odd? As though he is here with us…but he isn't. It makes me feel…" I don't even know what word to use though so many come to mind, spied upon, manipulated. I settle on "strange."

Pierre-Louis comes up behind me and presses a kiss to my shoulder. "It should make you feel loved, cherished. He cares enough about you that he wants you to feel special. He gives you permission to let nature take its course tonight, to bring the three of us closer together."

I duck away from his touch. "I don't like it. I don't like the way I am feeling right now."

He frowns at me. "How do you feel?"

I shrug, not sure, only knowing I don't like it. Maybe I am too tired and too sore from straddling the torturously narrow bicycle seat all morning. Maybe I am grumpy because both men assume nature taking its course means I will be naked in Pierre-Louis' arms before midnight. I sigh, knowing it is both. I am exhausted and I don't like being taken for granted.

"Put on the dress, *Belle*."

I shake my head. "I don't think I want to. I'm too tired for dinner anyway."

He approaches me slowly, with a sinfully seductive swagger, or maybe the swagger is just in my mind. Sinful and seductive is just the way he is, 24/7/365. He puts his hands on either shoulder and gazes deep into my eyes. "I'm starving, it's been a long, hard day and my ass hurts. It's been a long time since I've put in that many hours on a bike, but I think dinner will make me feel better, more human, and I'm asking you to join me for a meal, not because François expects me to fall on you like an animal when I see how enticing the dress makes you, but because I would like companionship at my table. If you insist on wearing the towel instead of the dress, so be it."

I look away, embarrassed, and hold my hand out for the hanger. He hands me the dress and I go back into the bathroom to get dressed for diner.

* * * * *

I start my meal with pan-seared scallops and dried citrus fruits served with a fresh herb salad and a red pepper gazpacho topped with Bavarian garlic cream. He has an aumônière of smoked duck breast encasing eggs scrambled with chanterelle mushrooms served with a plate of stewed tomatoes and lamb's lettuce drizzled with walnut oil. We both have red wine, a Petit Montibeau. Can I really stay irritated? Marvelous food…award-winning wine…sitting in the enclosed terrace listening to soft music, overlooking rolling hills as the sun sets on the horizon?

"You have two daughters?"

I look at him and realize I know nothing about him, and he knows only what Frankie has shared with him about me. "Yes, Ells and Bree." I tilt my head, amending, "Elizabeth and Brianna. They are twins, identical in every way, but sometimes when I look at them I see more of myself in Ellie and more of John in Bree."

He smiles and nods. "I suppose it would be normal for them to each pick up different traits."

Our main course arrives and we stop talking, that the waiter may set the plates in front of us. I am served the shellfish ravioli with a leek fondue and ginger cream, and he the roasted quail, drizzled with Cognac and grape gravy served with pear compote lightly spiced with fresh ground nutmeg.

"*Magnifique*," he pronounces as he tastes the compote. "I must learn this."

I taste the spoonful he offers and roll my eyes. "Food should not be this good."

Conversation ceases while we eat and when we finish, there is an awkward silence. I fill it in with, "That was amazing."

"I hope you have room for something sweet."

"Dessert?" I ask, saying, "No. I couldn't." But then the waiter arrives bearing a tray laden with supreme decadence and choosing becomes difficult. No common cheesecake here. No, it is iced chestnut parfait served with vanilla cream with a hint of rum and a hazelnut dacquoise, or mango shortbread served with a pineapple and fresh mint salsa and a passion fruit sorbet topped with a red fruit espuma, or a chocolate torte served with a warm, rich fudge sauce and a white chocolate ganache. I finally choose the shortbread, he picks the parfait. We taste each other's, agreeing when we finish the last bite we must take an evening walk to relieve the gluttonous bloat.

"Oh God." I say, stepping out of the restaurant. "I could spend the entire holiday here…just eating."

He laughs. "I think it is a good thing we ride tomorrow."

My backside argues to the contrary.

He takes my hand and leads me down a dark walking path to the grounds' massive medieval gardens. Crickets lend music to the warm night. My heart starts pounding with their rhythm. I had been able to put the night and all that comes with darkness out of my mind for most of the day. I know Frankie said intimacy…sex…wasn't a requirement, but damn, to deny I want to experience what this twenty-eight-year-old can do in the bedroom would be a bold-faced lie. In the darkness I bite my lip, letting him pull me through a low-growing bayberry maze. In the shadowy darkness of a corner, he comes to a stop and pulls me against him. He lowers his head to kiss me, I tilt my face up with no doubt we will kiss, no doubt what the kisses will lead to, Strangely I'm okay with the thought and equally strangely I don't feel manipulated by Frankie.

His lips are warm and knowledgeable, his kisses drawing moans from my throat.

I try to be quiet but need bursts through me. I want him, desperately. I have wanted him since the first time I laid eyes on him. I push my hands under his jacket, wanting to get closer to his skin. He stills my wrists, stopping me.

"I want to touch you."

"Shh, let's go to the room."

"Says the brave guy who wanted to lay me down in a field of mustard today."

He leans very close to my face and whispers, "We didn't have an audience then."

I still, forcing myself not to jerk my head around looking. If he thinks someone is watching, I believe him. I let him pull me through the maze, catching hushed whispers and giggles of others hidden among the hedges. "I didn't even hear them," I admit.

"I'm all for an audience sometimes," he admits, "but not tonight. Tonight I want to get to know you. I want to learn what pleasures your body."

His words make me tingle, my need mounting. I was ready to rip off his clothes, not caring if it pleased my whole body, just one small part. By the time we reach our room though, the moment has passed, and I am nervous and on edge. I know the exact moment he is going to kiss me and I swallow hard, wetting my lips in anticipation.

"I want to make love to you, *Belle*."

I open my mouth to agree and he commands the moment, kissing me with a fierceness I hadn't expected. Fierce yet gentle, his passion stealing my breath, the softness of his lips and tongue making it impossible to think. I remember Frankie saying to me that he fucks as well as he kisses. I think if that is really true I may not survive the night.

He wraps his hand into my hair, pulling me closer, forcing me to stay with the kiss, as though I might want to pull away. It is a dominating move and I wonder if that is the way it is to be then, me topped by two men. I close my mind against the earlier fantasy of me topping him, but then I wonder why. Why shouldn't I have the opportunity to top him?

I wrap my hand into his hair, my fingers mean as I jerk his head back, gaining his gaze. I lift my lips close, closer, but not touching his, and when he tries to move closer, tries to touch our lips, I hold him back, feeling the build of sexual tension between us as we both fight to control. We both plan to top.

Quite suddenly, he releases me. "*Bonne nuit.*"

I frown as he walks away and watch as he enters the suite next door. "Did I just miss something?"

First and foremost, I'm American. Maybe that explains why I don't do nuances well. I follow him and pound on the door. As the door opens, it vaguely registers that he looks relieved. I demand, "What just happened?"

His mouth opens and shuts but he doesn't explain anything. I step closer, pushing my hand against his chest. His heart is racing beneath my palm.

"Don't you want me, Pierre-Louis?"

"Yes," he whispers back and I feel the dynamic beginning to shift. He is suddenly shy, almost bashful.

I push the door shut with a backward kick of my heel and lean in to kiss him. With my lips against his mouth, I demand, "How badly?"

"Desperately."

I arch my brow at him. "Really?"

"I am not permitted to coerce my way into your bed."

"Coerce?"

"Or seduce."

My brow furrows. "I must make the initial move?"

"*Oui.*"

"Didn't I already do that in the maze?"

"Who led whom?" he asks, looking forlorn. "I pulled you into my arms. You did not initiate our first kiss."

"And you will be punished for this breach on our return?"

He nods and I jerk his head back, commanding, "Kneel."

He does, surprisingly, and I have a moment's panic. I let go of his hair. *Oh shit, now what?*

"You're trembling" he says.

Great. He noticed. "I want you to make no mistake when you report back to Frankie. I am starting *this*." I admit, "I've never topped before. I just know that tonight, for this to work, I need to be in control."

"And you are afraid you will not be able to finish what you start?"

"Yes," I squeak.

He bows his head. "I am at your service, Mistress. You need only tell me what you require me to do."

I nod, need sizzling through me. I cannot remember ever being this horny. "I don't even know where to start."

"May I assist you with your dress?" he asks.

I lick my lips and nod, turning my back to him to give him access to the zipper. Behind me, I know the moment he stands and steps forward. It seems as if some electrical field sizzles between us, letting me feel his every move even though I cannot see him. I feel the warmth of his hand through the fabric as he unzips me, the cooler room air teasing my bare skin as it is exposed inch by inch. I shiver as the fabric falls open and starts to slide off my body. He controls the chiffon's fall, helping me to step from the fabric.

I am wearing only thigh highs and my stilettos when I turn to face him. "I did not give you permission to rise." Oh shit. Where did that come from? I don't know that I like the tone of my voice. It seems alien and peculiar.

He drops to his knees without hesitation. "My apologies, Mistress."

He is still wearing his suit and tie, and I appreciate the view of him all buttoned up and dashing. I do not expect him to return an appreciative gaze. I grab his hair at the crown and pull his face into the juncture of my thighs. "Do you want this?"

He pushes his face deeper and I jerk his head back. "Yes, Mistress," he answers.

I push my pelvis toward him, teasing while I still hold his hair in a tight grip. He nudges forward, his nose pushing between my thighs. His cheeks are rough where his five-o'clock shadow scrapes against my sensitive inner thighs.

"Permission to lick your clit, Mistress?"

God, yes. The flesh in question jumps at the suggestion, fully agreeable. I don't answer immediately, even though I think we're well past the point of stopping what we started. My mind travels to Frankie, and I feel I am betraying him. It seems to me he would not want Pierre-Louis topping me. It would stand to reason he also would not want me to top Pierre-Louis. "Don't call me Mistress, okay?"

"As you wish."

I separate my legs just enough to give him access. His tongue flicks out like a snake's and taps my clitoris. I flinch and his hands go around the backs of my thighs.

His voice is gentling and confident when he says, "Easy, *Belle.*"

Belle. Beautiful.

I like that he is not calling me Cassiopeia, though Charlotte or Charley would have been fine. I smile softly, thinking *Belle* is better than Mistress.

I tremble beneath the touch of his hands. His tongue flicks out again. Tapping. Tapping. I close my eyes when he licks, pleasure stabbing through me, making me gasp. My knees threaten to buckle. His grip on my thighs is tight as he pulls me against his mouth, his licks taking on a rhythm. Pleasure weaves around my clit, making it pulse. I find my need heightening, spiraling as I climb a familiar peak. "Oh God." I spasm against his lips and tongue. He keeps stroking, keeps pushing my need higher, until I am jerking with each electricity-filled touch. "Ah. Ah. Ahh." I gasp and buck against him, finally screaming, "Stop. Stopstopstop. I can't take any more."

He pulls his face away and I shake where I stand. He keeps his hands on the backs of my thighs and I am certain it is only his support that keeps me from falling. I think he waits for me to command him to do something…

"May I stand?" he asks.

"Please," I say, thankful he thought of it.

I put my hands on his suit jacket-covered chest and ask, "Help me to the bed?"

"My pleasure, *Belle*."

He surprises me by lifting me into his arms and carrying me to the bed. He lowers me gently and gives me a questioning look. I think I should have undressed him while we were standing. I could have slid his suit coat off his shoulders, untied his tie. I could have unbuttoned his shirt and unhooked his belt. "Take off your clothes. I want to see you naked. Slowly."

Watching him is better than helping him, I decide as he slides out of the jacket and folds it before laying it on a chair. He slides off his tie and tosses it to me. I think we both have the same idea—it might come in handy. He unbuttons his shirt, slowly and deliberately exposing each inch of muscled chest. I inhale a shuddered breath. He is more exquisite each time I look at him.

He steps out of his shoes and lowers his slacks. He saves his thong for last. Am I surprised he is wearing a thong? No. With a body like his, he should never wear more than a thong. He steps closer and I hold out a hand to lead him to the bed, seeing his erection is strained. He is so hard, I wonder if it hurts. He takes my hands and a single step forward, commanding, "Roll over."

I frown. "Don't try to top me."

"I wouldn't dream of it, *Belle*, only offering a suggestion." He lifts a challenging eyebrow. "Ask me to fuck you from behind...like an animal. Demand I fuck you as you've never been fucked before, *Belle*."

My heart leaps into my throat. I forget to breathe but I manage to roll over on to my stomach and push myself up on to my knees. "Fuck me, Pierre-Louis."

He grabs my hips and pulls me to the edge of the bed so that my legs drop over the side, then steps between my legs. I hear foil tearing and turn my head to watch him roll the condom down his length. He pushes his weight against me, bending over me, but he doesn't thrust inside, not yet. I feel his hand move between my legs, his fingers rubbing my slick slit. He draws my moisture in and around before sliding his finger inside me. I push back against him, "Now, please, Pierre-Louis."

He fingers me, alternating thrusts, soft slides with harder thrusts. I push back against his hand, anxious for more. He draws my wetness over my clit and swirls its head, making me cry out. He pulls the fluid back along my slit, all the way to my anus and I shy away from his touch. He gentles me, "Sh-sh-sh, relax. I won't take you here," making certain I understand exactly what we're talking about by sweeping his fingers in a teasing arc around the rim, "until you command it. But let me play a little. When you come I want it to be like fireworks going off in your body. An explosion of pleasure, *oui*?"

"I want you inside of me," I say.

"A bit longer, *ma belle*. Let me play a bit longer."

I feel his erection slide between my ass cheeks, rubbing, not penetrating, as his fingers go back to rubbing my clit. Oh God.

I let him have his way, playing, teasing with his fingers every slick needy place between clit and asshole, making me want and need enough to beg. "Please, please, please."

"You want me inside of you then?"

"Yes. Fuck me."

I feel his penis push against the opening of my vagina and I thrust back, forcing him in. He pushes deeper and then even deeper, until I am full. He withdraws a little, then thrusts in again.

"Not gently, Pierre-Louis. Fuck me like you mean it."

Grabbing my hips, he pulls me back on his length as he thrusts forward. It hurts, it feels amazing, and I think I babble a little incoherently under my breath. He thrusts again, pushing as hard as he can against the solid wall inside, making me scream and moan.

"Faster. Harder."

He honors my request, thrusting harder, deeper, faster…the whole time rolling my clit between his finger and thumb, leaving me gasping, panting. I spasm against his hand, coming, but he doesn't stop thrusting.

He works me into a second frenzy, but my body won't climb high enough to spiral back down. I need more.

"Ask for it, *ma belle*."

We both know what he is asking.

I shake my head, not from fear or some feeling of taboo, but because no one has ever gone back door on me except for Master. I don't know how he would feel, I don't know how I feel…

He pulls his penis out of my vagina and I moan at the loss of fullness inside my body. He rubs its slick head against my anus. My body responds, pushing back, wanting, needing, but he doesn't penetrate. He leans his weight over me, his chest hot, damp and heavy against my back. He whispers against my cheek, "We won't do anything you aren't comfortable with."

My mouth responds to my need, begging. "Please, Pierre-Louis, I need to come again."

"*Oui*, I want you to." He rubs my clit harder but we both know I need to be filled, I need the sensation that comes with being filled in my ass.

"Doitdoitdoit," I beg.

"It?" he teases.

"Fuck me in the ass, Pierre-Louis, and do it like you mean it, damn you."

He chuckles and teases my rim with his fingertips, drawing moisture from my sopping pussy as he does so. Aching with desire, I push back against his fingers. Slowly he answers my need, pushing into me with first his finger, then two fingers, loosening me, making me see stars, making my body quake. He finally pushes in the head, waiting for my body to adjust. "Give me your hands, *Belle*."

I bring my hands down to my sides.

"Hold open your ass cheeks."

I do as he asks, feeling naughty, dirty, slutty…and incredibly turned-on, all at the same time. His request twists something in my head, making everything rev up a notch.

He pushes his length in deeper, still rolling my clit between his fingers.

"Feel me entering you with your fingertips, *ma belle*, know I am feeding your dark hole my cock."

I feel, I hold myself open, but I also feel his length sliding through my fingers. He thrusts. In. Out. In. Out. The sensation is mind-stretching, my entire body responding to each stroke. I start to come, but I want him there as well. I beg, "Come in me, Pierre-Louis. Come for me now."

He pushes in hard, forcing a small scream from my throat. My orgasm washes over me and through me, a tidal wave of sensation. My clit spasms, my vagina clenches and my ass contracts. It is as if three distinct orgasms are crashing over my body simultaneously. I hear him over me, his ravaged breathing, his pants. He moans against me, going still. I buck against him as fast and hard as my hips will bounce, until I am coming again. "Ohhhhhhmmmmmmyyyyyggggooodddd."

I think we are through and I collapse under his weight, crawling up and into the bed only after he stands and moves away. When he rolls me over and pushes the hair out of my face, I see he has pulled off his condom but is unrolling a fresh one. Really?

"You wish to still fuck, *oui*?"

I nod, wide-eyed as he crawls between my legs, dons a fresh condom and guides his erection into me. I am left speechless and wondering why I hadn't considered a younger man all those nights I was lying alone knowing John was with one of his students...

* * * * *

I awake to sunlight streaming in through an open window and the sound of a shower running. I sit up, thinking I will join Pierre-Louis in the shower but my body protests, every single muscle screaming. I push the covers off my legs and it is with some effort I throw them over the sides of the bed. This is ridiculous. We didn't bicycle that far. I'm not this out of shape, am I? I hear the water shut off and panic. I cannot let him see me struggling to get out of bed. I hurry to push off the mattress and stand, fighting back a shriek as my calf muscles take my weight. Oh God.

I hurry across the room, saying "ouch" with each step.

Pierre-Louis comes out of the bathroom scrubbing his hair with a towel. He is nude and perfect and so fucking young. I feel like a train ran over me in the night.

He sees I am awake and, smiling widely, comes to my side to pull me into his arms. "*Belle*, you slept well?"

"Yes."

He kisses me softly and I startle when I hear a soft rap at the door. "Room service," he explains. "You were sleeping so sweetly, I wanted to surprise you."

I smile. "I'm surprised. Mind if I shower first?"

"Of course. Go, go."

While he is dealing with room service, I hurry out of sight, my legs and ass muscles screaming with each step. I hope a shower helps because I see no way of sitting on that damn narrow seat a second day in a row. I hear him talking as I turn on the shower and step inside. The warm water is a balm and I close my eyes, only opening them when I feel his hands massaging shampoo through my tresses.

He steps inside the stall with me and rubs my scalp. It feels wonderful. "I told the tour leader we would not be cycling today. I hope you are not too disappointed."

He rinses my hair and I open my eyes. "Did I oversleep?"

"We overslept. I thought the alarm was set…but no."

If I could manage it, I would jump up and down. As it is I contain my excitement. "I loved yesterday, but I'm sure we can find something to do to entertain ourselves today, right?"

He smiles. "If I can lie in bed naked with you today, it will be a day well spent."

I tilt my head to kiss him, agreeing, "Very, very, well spent," as he kisses me with deliberate slowness.

I am not surprised when he pushes me up against the cool tile wall, or when he pushes his fingers through my slick folds, or even when he lifts me. I am surprised when my body doesn't rebel and my muscles don't scream in pain as he impales me. Holding me against the wall, he lifts my ankles up to his shoulders so that I am bent in half. He pounds into me, I pound into the tile. My clit is crushed between our bodies on each thrust and released on each withdrawal. I am panting and screaming, my fingernails run down his back, tearing a groan from his throat. He pounds harder and I bite down on his shoulder, liking the roughness, needing him to be rougher. He bites too, holding my shoulder in a firm grip between his teeth as he pounds me senseless. My vagina contracts around him and he shudders, growling like a wild beast.

Spent, we cling to each other, warm water sluicing over us.

I wipe his shoulder, realizing I drew blood. I don't know whether to apologize or say nothing. He asks, "Are you okay? I wasn't too rough?"

He lowers me to the ground and I can barely stand. "Not too rough. Besides, I should be asking you that. You're the one bleeding."

He laughs at me, asking, "You have met François' cane, *oui?*"

Chapter Ten

🕉

We don't leave our room but I do call Frankie. In a pinch and out of condoms, I try to think of a polite way to ask him if they are fluid bonded. This isn't a conversation I am ready for once I have him on the phone.

"You sound stressed, what is wrong?"

Pierre-Louis kisses a path from my breasts to my clit, flicking out his tongue to make me jump. I almost shriek into the phone, "Nothing."

"Yes, there is something. You have only been away thirty-six hours. Tell me you do not hate each other."

"We don't hate each other."

Pierre-Louis slides his tongue through my folds, making my breath catch and I gasp softly. Using my knee, I try to nudge him away so I can actually have this conversation.

"Ha," Frankie cries out, "I know that sound. He is between your legs, *oui*?"

He sounds positively overjoyed.

"Yes," I admit.

"Then what is the problem. American morals? You must call me first to make certain I am okay with the two of you fucking?" He laughs. "Please, fuck. Fuck like bunnies in the springtime."

The visual is overwhelming.

"That's the problem. We have no condoms."

The line goes silent.

"We had condoms, but now we are out. Pierre-Louis is trying to convince me that since the two of you are fluid bonded and have been exclusive for almost a decade and because you have both been tested regularly…that it would be safe for the three of us to be fluid bonded. I realize over the phone isn't the best way to have this conversation."

I stop babbling because a moan fills my throat. Pierre-Louis intent on distracting me. He pushes a second finger inside my vagina to join the first in creating havoc with my G-spot.

"I wish you were here."

"Me too," he whispers. "To see your face right now. To see Pierre-Louis'. *Mon dieu.*"

I close my eyes, having one lover on the phone and one lover between my legs stretching my limit on how much I can take. Frankie makes a sound in the back of his throat and I know he is touching himself. "Tell me what he is doing."

"He is stroking my G-spot with his fingers."

"Ahh," he sighs. "And you are enjoying it?"

"You haven't been listening to my moans?"

"We are fluid bonded. We have been for seven years. If you choose to enjoy him bareback, it will be fine. But I will expect the same privilege when you return."

"Of … ahhhhh … course." My back arches when Pierre-Louis licks his tongue over my clit. I am embarrassed by the sounds I make in my throat and tell Frankie, "I should go."

"Hang up?" he asks, demanding, "No. I want to hear. Put the phone on speaker and enjoy him, but do not disconnect."

I do as I am asked, feeling more self-conscious, but then I admit to Pierre-Louis, "We have Frankie's blessing."

He lifts his face and smiles. He crawls over me, touching his lips to mine. My scent is on his face and I taste myself on his lips. For whatever reason, the two combined make me crazed. I want him. Need. Him. I try to hurry him with kisses, grabbing his length in my hand to guide him in, but he angles away. "A moment as precious as this cannot be rushed, *ma belle.*"

I pout, lifting my hips to try to force the issue. He nods at the phone. "He's listening?"

"Yes."

He smiles and it is wicked. I'm not certain what he has planned until he pushes my legs over my head, bending me in half. "Hold your ankles and do not let go."

As long as it gets his dick inside me, I would agree to anything. I am savage with need and don't understand why every time he fills me, every time he makes me come, I only want him twice as badly...again.

He fills me with a deep thrust, making me cry out, and my pleasure is tamped down by thinking too much about Frankie listening. Pierre-Louis pushes my legs further, stretching muscles I've probably never stretched, ever, but when he kisses me, filling my mouth with his tongue, I forget the pain and my climax shoots me to the moon.

It is many minutes before I remember Master is on the phone. "Are you still there?"

"*Oui*, though feeling a bit forgotten."

"Never, Master." I sit up. "I was only catching my breath."

"And perhaps I would have heard you panting as you report on my lover's expertise."

My heart lodges in my throat. It seems Frankie has gone from pleased to peeved in a very short time, but then I remember what it was like to listen outside the door. I release a long, slow breath, hoping he doesn't hear the exhalation. "He was everything you promised and more. Thank you for the opportunity to experience him, Master."

I watch Pierre-Louis leave the bed and disappear into the bathroom. He looks less happy than Master sounds. *Shit.* "Are we all right, Master?"

"Are we?"

"I am more committed to you and the lifestyle we share than I ever have been. I love you. I respect you." It seems there is so much more I could say and like I've already said everything wrong. I whisper, "I wish you were here beside me right now. I wish you were here to hold me."

"Then we are all right, Cassiopeia. *Faites des beaux rêves. Je pense à toi, toute la nuit.*"

Crap. My French is so rusty. I think he said sweet dreams and… something about night. I love you seems a reasonable response, right? "*Je t'aime.*"

He hangs up without saying anything else.

I throw the phone across the room and it lands in a chair. Too bad it didn't crash into the wall and fall in a million pieces. I bury my face in my hands.

"He wanted this to happen between us."

I look up to see Pierre-Louis leaning against the wooden doorjamb between rooms.

"So everyone keeps saying."

"You don't believe him?"

"I think he thought he wanted it and now that it's happened — maybe it was a mistake."

Pierre-Louis crosses the room and joins me on the bed. "I don't believe that."

He smells of shampoo and sweet lavender soap. "What does '*Faites des beaux rêves. Je pense à toi, toute la nuit*' mean?"

"This is what he said, *oui*?"

I nod.

"Then he told you 'sweet dreams' and 'I will think of you all night.' It is nothing to worry about."

Then why am I so worried?

* * * * *

We wake up early and drive to the next stop on the bike tour, collect our bikes and start riding. Though staying in bed all day would have been preferable, I can't say I am up to another day of marathon sex. But on the same note, my body, or rather my pussy, isn't up to a whole day on a bike either.

I am a true masochist.

After three hours, I know my limits as such.

I hobble to a large rock under a tree and sit. Pierre-Louis brings me a boxed lunch filled with gourmet goodies only the French can conjure. I eat, closing my eyes as my taste buds dance in delight.

"We can take the shadow van to the hotel."

"Do I look that miserable?" I open my eyes to find him nodding.

"There's no shame in knowing your limits."

"I'm not sore from the bike."

"I know."

I agree to ride to the next hotel and we check in to a single room. I announce, "I'm soaking in a tub."

Pierre-Louis doesn't acknowledge. After carrying in the bags, he drops on to the bed like a stone. I think he's asleep before his head even hits the pillow. *So much for the marathon-man twenty-eight year old.*

* * * * *

I feel much better after a long soak and Pierre-Louis' power nap seems to have revitalized him. I don't bother with clothes and it isn't hard to get him out of his. I lose track of how many times I peak, but know for a fact Pierre-Louis has ejaculated six times. He was going along with a two-to-one deal but then he made me come a third time before he did and after that all deals were out the window and now he strives to break a world record. I don't think the number of climaxes a woman has had in a day is a category with the folks at

Guinness but dissuading Pierre-Louis is too difficult. Plus, I don't care.

We have dinner brought up by room service. I'm too damn happy, which I comment on randomly. "I feel stoned."

"Stoned?"

"Blurry, disconnected, higher than a goddamn kite. I think your spunk is infused with mind-altering drugs."

"Oh, I have heard of this, *oui*. Like chocolate."

"Chocolate isn't a mind-altering drug."

"No, but if you overindulge you will feel high."

I laugh at him, rolling over on to my back to twist my own nipples. My distraction tactic works. Sort of. He lowers his mouth to take my nipple into his mouth. I writhe, my nipple seemingly attached to my uterus, his suck making my womb spasm, needy. He says around the soft pink flesh, "It was an article in *Time* magazine. Chocolate goes to the same brain receptors as THC."

"Marijuana?"

"*Oui.* And so it is like too much sex. I think if you are feeling stoned, you have had too much for one day."

I laugh at him, wrapping my hands around his face to pull him closer. I kiss him, asking, "Are you ready to sleep then?"

He smiles coyly. "Not likely."

When my cell phone rings, I jump to answer it, thinking it is Ells and Bree. My heart sinks, seeing it is Master. I drop the phone back into my purse. "I can't do this again tonight."

"Was that wise?"

"You want to call him back?"

"Not really."

"Good." I caress his face. "Where were we?"

"Kissing."

"Then why aren't you kissing me?"

His lips descend on mine and Master is forgotten in a rush of pheromones.

* * * * *

Morning comes too soon and we both wake up quiet. Is it because we know we are going back to the château…and Frankie? I'm not sure why that should matter though. I find myself packing slowly and sighing a lot. I won't deny I am worried about the dynamic of our relationships, mine and Frankie's, mine and Pierre-Louis', and of course the three of us and how we interact together. I also worry about the consequences of not answering Master's call yesterday and worry that it is worse because he didn't call back, although at the time I was glad he didn't. Irritated, I sit on the bed by my bag and watch Pierre-Louis fold shirts. "Why did we do this? Why did we come here together? What in the hell did Frankie expect?"

"It wasn't Frankie's idea. You must know that. I told him I wanted time alone with you to see what would happen…to let nature take its course."

"Well, that was stupid."

"Was it?"

He's right. One way or another this would have eventually happened. There's too much attraction. Too much chemistry.

"Why would he agree?"

Pierre-Louis kneels in front of me. "If he fought me I would have become even more determined and the consequences—" He shrugs, making me wonder what he thought the consequences might be. Obviously, we all want the ménage to work, and if jealousy entered the picture, it wouldn't.

Looking down at my hands, I mull it over a bit before looking at him. "I have to know, although I shouldn't ask…" I shake my head, not sure whether I really want to ask or not.

Pierre-Louis takes my hand and encourages me with his eyes. I square my shoulders, bracing for his answer. "When you are together, which one of you is dominant?"

He smiles and laughs. "Do you really have to ask that? You've seen me naked and collared."

I nod, thinking too hard. "But behind closed doors—"

He smirks, squeezing my hand. "You want to know which one of us…er…pitches and which of us catches."

I snort and shake my head, blushing eight shades of crimson. "Yes, I guess that's my question. Who fucks whom?"

He sits back in his seat, withdrawing his hand, and I feel I have offended him. He looks thoughtful, weighing how his answer will affect the outcome of our holiday. I hurriedly say, "It isn't going to change what I think, or how I feel about you…either way."

"I am not so sure about that." His lips twitch. "As it is now, Frankie is your Master, he is my Master, and that is a very powerful dynamic. If you knew for a fact that I sometimes fuck him up the ass, it might very well change how you see him—and I do not want that."

I swallow, realizing that I have been too bold, too curious. I'm not so certain I do want the answer.

"On the other hand, I do wish to top you at some point and if you see no strength in me whatsoever, if you only see me as the weaker of the two—"

I interrupt quickly, grabbing his hand. "There is nothing about you that is weak. Nothing."

He squeezes my hand. "I need you to trust me, because I do want you to know that if you give me your submission I will cherish it, and so I will tell you the truth of this despite my fears. François always tops. Always. And I would have it no other way."

I swallow, not sure how knowing the truth does make me feel. I do see Pierre-Louis as very strong, very assured…very male. And to know this…I look at him, seeing both fear and hope in his eyes…changes nothing. I sigh, shifting in my seat.

"I didn't top him from below, if that is what you are worried about. We discussed what I was feeling. This seemed a reasonable answer to an unpleasant situation."

"Unpleasant?"

"Me, longing after you like a lust-filled schoolboy."

"Ahh."

"I'm sure it was obvious."

"Perhaps to Master, not to me."

"Yes, well, he *knows* me."

I remember what our original intent was supposed to have been and begin to think we could have made better use of our time instead of just having sex.

"We fucked away our time," I say. "We should have at least exchanged stories, gotten to know each other."

He tilts my chin in his hand. "Do not look so disheartened, *mon amour*. We are learning each other. But I do not understand this—stories?"

"From your childhood. From your teenage years. What has made you *you*?"

"That is too much for a single weekend, *ma belle*. It would require a lifetime to share so much. What is something easy you wish to know?"

"Your birthday."

"February first. What is your worry?"

"Master sent us away to get to know each other better. I know no more about you than when we left the château."

"*Non*, he sent us away together to allow us to *bond*." He kisses me, a quick peck before standing to finish folding and packing. If he meant for his words to be reassuring, they weren't.

* * * * *

If I felt strange driving away from the château and Frankie three days ago, returning is stranger still, but when I see him standing on the stoop, waiting, smiling, I know that somehow everything will be okay. I squeeze Pierre-Louis' hand before I step from the car. Frankie kisses me on both cheeks. "You had a good holiday?"

I blush. "Yes, thank you."

Pierre-Louis joins us and Frankie kisses him on both cheeks as well. "*Bienvenue.*"

We walk into the house together. Frankie turns to us both, commanding, "Disrobe."

Oh. Shit. Every bruise comes to mind, both the ones I left on Pierre-Louis and the ones he left on me. Well, on with it then. It's easy enough to undress. I wore a sleeveless cotton-jersey dress that I can pull over my head, which leaves me wearing solely peep-toe black pumps. No bra. No panties. No thigh-high stockings. Pierre-Louis takes a bit longer, but not too much, polo shirt, khakis, thong underwear and leather loafers with no socks. He strips out of everything.

Standing in the foyer, sun streaming in through the still-open front door, we are spotlighted and I see Frankie's eyes widen appreciatively at the long tracks of welts I made down Pierre-Louis' back. He traces one. "Fingernails."

He touches the scabbed-over bite mark I left on Pierre-Louis' shoulder. "Teeth."

He looks at the large black-and-blue mark on his ass. His eyebrows arch. "Paddle?"

Pierre-Louis' lips twitch. "I wish. I was showing off and fell off my bike."

"Ah. *Oui.*"

He points at the road rash on his thigh and calf. "Obviously."

He circles me. For the most part I am unmarked, bruising on my shoulder from a lover's bite. He taps it. "A hickey? That's it? And I thought that Pierre-Louis was my more passionate lover."

I frown. I'm not as passionate as Pierre-Louis? I don't have any time to dwell on that though because the next thing Frankie says is, "Dungeon. Now."

Any time Master says the words dungeon and now in that tone I know that there is soon hell to pay. My heart starts racing and I don't even think, I go, I hurry to the stairs leading down. I've never seen the dungeon here, but I know what to expect having seen the one he keeps in a modern basement in Chicago. Hitting the bottom step, I am not disappointed. I do not know how old the château is but the dungeon seems to have been here since the dawn of time. Stone walls, stone floor, wrought iron pieces meant to hold torches and candles. On the left we have the wine cellar and on the right—

Wow. I'm stunned. It appears Frankie is a collector of mint-condition antique torture devices. Iron cages, a rack, yokes, stocks and implements I have no name for and am not certain I want to be introduced to. I hope they are for ambiance, not usage.

It takes me a moment to realize I am alone and I only notice that I am not accompanied by Frankie or Pierre-Louis when I hear them arguing upstairs. Obviously Pierre-Louis is made of stern stuff. I want to go back upstairs but I won't. The marks from the caning on the night of my return are only just faded.

"You didn't even attempt to top her?"

"*Non.*"

"But you allowed her to top you?"

"*Non.*"

"What do you mean? *Non, non?*"

"We fucked, that is all."

"You, fucking her, left these marks?" He runs his fingertips over a raised red line that runs the length of Pierre-Louis' back.

"*Oui.*"

"I don't believe you."

"We fucked like bunnies, that is all."

I hear Pierre-Louis moan and I can imagine that Frankie has pinched one of the welts I left down his back. "Did she gain pleasure seeing her mark on you?"

"You would have to ask her."

"*Oui,* I will," Frankie agrees. "I am not certain I like seeing her mark on you."

My anxiety level triples, realizing Frankie has issues. I left marks on Pierre-Louis. I had considered it would not be wise if Pierre-Louis left marks on me, because Frankie is a very possessive man, but I am not sure why I didn't consider he would be as possessive of Pierre-Louis. Oh hell. Hearing a footfall on the stairs, I wish I could hide, but I stand at attention, waiting, palms sweating, heart pounding, adrenaline pulsing forcefully through my veins. He will blame me...for all of it. For enticing Pierre-Louis, for leaving the marks on him, for not answering the phone. An excuse to punish me, though in truth he needs no excuse at all.

I remember this from when we were together before. Although the cane was rarely used, there are many ways to punish a person's body. Some are enjoyable, some are not. It seems like forever since I returned to Master and yet it has been only a week. And in truth, my time alone with Pierre-Louis has taken most of it.

Master instructs Pierre-Louis to wait upstairs. "I think you have forgotten what it means to belong to me, *ma cherie.*"

I swallow hard. *Ma cherie.* My darling. This is bad. This is very bad. In the past, the only time he used that endearment was when he was going to hurt me very, very bad.

"You have enjoyed looking at my collection?"

133

I lick my lips nervously. "It is very impressive."

"*Oui,*" he agrees. He walks over to the corner and picks up a wooden stock which is obviously not an antique. Bringing it over to me he lowers the top half onto my neck and brings the bottom half up to meet it, locking the two parts together. I slide my hands through the three holes so that I am carrying it on my shoulders like a yoke. I take a deep breath, trying hard to remain silent…because he is.

He attaches a leather cuff to each wrist, which he then attaches to the stock, making it impossible to slide my hands back out. He attaches a chain to each end of the stock. A pulley rewinds the chain until I am where he wants me to be—on tiptoe.

"Is that comfortable?" he asks.

"Not really, Master."

"Hmm," he says. "Do you think I want you to be comfortable?"

"No, Master."

He lowers the chain, feeding out length until I am flat on my feet again, but then he continues to feed chain, saying, "Bend forward."

I bend as the chain feeds until I am at an angle with the floor, bent at my thighs, not my waist.

"Better?" he asks.

I exhale, relieved. "Yes, Master."

"Good. I want you to think a while about what it means to belong to me."

I do not expect him to walk away, but that is exactly what he does. I am left hanging in the stocks, thinking how ridiculous. How childish. Wondering how long he intends to leave me to think.

I stare at the stone floor and it becomes apparent fairly quickly that the wooden contraption around my neck is going to grow very heavy, very fast, and that is a concern. My bigger concern is having nothing to think about. Not that I don't have plenty to think about, just that I don't want to think about any of it.

Damn it to hell.

I stubbornly, adamantly refuse to think.

I shuffle around, bent over, stuck in stocks, making a small rotation, trying to find something of interest to look at to keep my mind from thinking about whatever it is he wants me to think about. A few minutes later I reverse my shuffle, focusing on the stone stairwell he just ascended. Better just to watch and wait for his return.

* * * * *

I shuffle, forward a few inches, backward a few inches. My back aches, my calves are screaming bloody murder. The wood on my shoulders officially weighs tons and I am getting angry. I don't deserve to be punished. I didn't do anything. I stare at the stone steps and wait...

* * * * *

Nodding off wakes me up immediately because it causes my throat to push into the wood around my neck, hurting, cutting off my air. I want to scream for Master to come down and release me. I want to talk about this like civilized grown-ups. Yes, I left marks on Pierre-Louis but what is the answer to that? I shouldn't have? It isn't as if I meant to. It isn't as if I purposely marked the man.

* * * * *

I'm not sure when I started crying but my face is wet when I hear Master descending the stairs. I do not want him to see my wet face, I do not want him to know I cried, but there is no way to hide the evidence, no way to wipe my face. It seems as though days have passed with me standing here but it has been only hours. I know this because I have stood days before and this doesn't compare. Uncomfortable but not unbearable, and not yet humiliating.

He comes up to me and bends to establish eye contact. "Are you comfortable?"

"Fine, Master."

He narrows his eyes at me before wiping his fingers through my tears. "Not in pain?"

"No, Master," I answer and a sharp pain stabs through my shoulder to remind me I am lying.

"Ah, Cassiopeia. You were always so willing to suffer for me a little. I was hoping your stubborn streak would have softened with time."

"I am who I am, Master."

He laughs. "I suppose you are."

We stare at each other until he stands. He asks, "Why did you return to me?"

I've wondered that myself. "Because I missed you."

"Missed me? Or missed the play?"

Play. Interesting that something sometimes painful and humiliating is called play. He has his back to me, having walked over to a workbench. I see that it is also a storage area for very adult toys. "I missed you…being yours…and what we did together."

"Can you agree a servant can only serve one Master?"

I blink, hating where this is going. He turns toward me carrying a riding crop.

"Pierre-Louis did not top me." I realize my mistake as soon as I say the words.

"But you topped him?"

"Only a little," I whisper.

He strikes my hip with the crop and the sting reverberates through my body. He strikes me again. "Did you get to know one another while you were on holiday?"

"Yes, Master."

"Really? So you can tell me where he was born? Perhaps his brothers' and sisters' names?"

I jerk, anticipating another strike, but the crop only caresses the inside of my thigh. I do not know where he was born or that he even has brothers and sisters. If he asks me his favorite color or favorite food I will not know the answer to that either. I am so screwed.

"What can you tell me about Pierre-Louis that you did not know before you went away on holiday with him?" He slides the crop up and down my inner thighs.

"His birthday is February first."

"What else?"

"You were right about him being an amazing fuck."

His laughter echoes around the room. "So you would like the privilege of being allowed to fuck him again?"

Oh God. Is this a trick question? "Yes, Master."

"So you would have no use for me then?"

All of my muscles tense at once. I wish my arms were free to throw around his neck. I wish I knew what he was thinking. Feeling. I know how I felt when I knew John was fucking women half my age and it wasn't pretty.

"No one can replace you, Master." I recall with complete clarity what being owned by François de Hart felt like. I was precious to him. He cherished me. He placed me before all else in his world and I did the same for him. No one has ever made me feel as needed or as protected as Frankie made me feel. It is an addictive thing. The more I pleased him, the more he praised me, the more I needed. I'm not a young girl needing praise and approval anymore, but a small voice in my head demands. "You are my world."

"I was not your world when you refused to answer my call last night."

He drops the riding crop at my feet and walks away, leaving me stunned. I wish he would just punish me and get it over with but as he climbs the stairs I begin to fear that whatever we shared before is long gone, never to be resurrected again.

* * * * *

Everything hurts. My lower back is a hell zone of pins and needles. My legs are on fire, every muscle from the tips of my toes to my thighs. My wrists and neck, immobilized for hours, ache with a dull pain that becomes excruciating when I make the mistake of moving them. My head pounds and I pissed myself. I remember this.

To say that you belong to a person is mere words. To accept the truth of it when it is proven takes a singular strength. Some people can, some people cannot. Frankie is rubbing my face in the fact I am his if I want to be. The question is, do I want to be?

Do I want my every thought and deed orchestrated?

Do I want to give up control of my life to suit his will?

As far as my boss in Chicago is concerned, I am on vacation, making the return to my old life fairly simple. Board a plane, go home, forget Frankie and Pierre-Louis and France…

I want out of these wooden stocks. That is all I care about. If I had to promise to go away and never set foot on French soil again, I would agree to it, though I hope that is not the option I am given.

Chapter Eleven

ɛɔ

Both men come down the stairs together. I'm not crying, I am stoic. Whatever is…is, whatever comes to be…does. Frankie comes forward but Pierre-Louis waits at the foot of the stairs. Even from a distance I can see fresh marks on his body. His head is bowed and his hands are clasped behind his back. He is a good little slave, waiting to be told what to do next. I'm not a good little slave. I accuse, "You wanted me to go on holiday with Pierre-Louis. You wanted to see how nature would take its course."

"*Oui.*"

"And now I am punished for allowing whatever was going to happen to happen?"

A surprised look is my answer. "You think I am punishing you for fucking with Pierre-Louis?"

"And for leaving him marked. Yes."

"Then you have remembered nothing." He comes closer, moving behind me. I can feel the heat of his body rising off him. His hand runs up my thigh, his fingers smooth over my labia, a single finger penetrates between my folds. "You are very wet, *ma cherie.*"

"Yes," I whimper as raw lust explodes through my core from his slight touch.

"You are wet for me?"

"Yes. Yes," I declare fervently, pushing against his fingers. He rewards me by rubbing through the folds to stroke my clit, making my knees buckle with the pleasure of it.

"You enjoy being the property of François de Hart."

Rhetorical, but I agree anyway. The whimpers forming in my throat that would have embarrassed me a week ago are now accepted as part of who I am...still...not the woman I once was, but the woman I am still.

"I am not punishing you, *mon amour*."

"No?" I ask, reveling in his soft touch between my legs. His caresses take my mind off the pain everywhere else. My world centers around my pussy and my clit each time he strokes it.

"I want you to remember what it means to belong to me."

"Yesssss," I sigh, my hips bucking against his hand.

"I want you to understand I will use you as I desire to. Pleasure, pain. If it is my will to leave you in the stocks day in and day out, I will do so. Do you understand?"

The memories return in a flood, the hours, days he left me alone, in the dark, sometimes tied, sometimes not, always feeling abandoned and forgotten, and the immeasurable joy each time he returned. *This was life with Master.* How is it over the years I've forgotten the horrors and humiliations and only romanticized the most intimate moments?

"If I choose to share you, I will share you. And if I choose to deny you ever experiencing another again, that is my right, my decision to make."

My eyes jerk up to Pierre-Louis, but his gaze stays stubbornly attached to the stonework beneath his bare toes.

Master's fingers penetrate my pussy, not one, fuller than one, two or three, and the fullness makes me moan, not with pleasure. I am reminded that Pierre-Louis and I may have indulged once or twice, or a dozen times too often. I back up to take in more but the pain in my back stops me, making me groan in pain.

"Too much sex with the one who is not your Master has left you too injured for my attentions?"

This is dangerous ground I tread.

"Can you override the discomfort of your body to come for *me*?"

"Yes, Master." I close my eyes. His desire seems an impossible task.

"If you come for me, I will release you now. If you do not, I will leave you strung up."

Oh shit. My heart drops into the pit of my stomach.

He instructs Pierre-Louis to bring him the Hitachi and he hurries to do as he is bade, handing him the vibrator then returning to his post, keeping watch on the floor. I shouldn't care what Pierre-Louis is doing. He shouldn't be even a small part of my focus.

Frankie moves the Hitachi against my clit and my world focuses on the single pinpoint of bliss. High-pitched barks spill from my throat. Frankie chastises, "I don't even believe it feels that good yet."

My body spirals up into a spinning vortex of pleasure, my body seems to levitate, all pain forgotten. I scream, "Yes. It. Does."

"You will tell me before you come."

I am already falling into the chasm, bliss speeding through my veins. I manage to scream, "Now. Oh god, now." He keeps the Hitachi centered on my clit, allowing wave after wave to crash through me. I scream, "Ahhahhhaaaaahhh. Ahhahhhaaaaaahhh. Ahhhahhhhaaaaaahhhh," but he doesn't release me from the pleasure or the pain as the Hitachi becomes torment. "Please, please, please," I beg. "Master, I'm done."

He says very clearly, "You are done when I say you are done, Cassiopeia. Come for me until I say stop."

The Hitachi feels like knife points on my supersensitive clit. I sob and beg. I feel his fingers push into my pussy. He pushes against my G-spot and I push back, pain raking through my bent spine. It hurts enough to make me forget the Hitachi on my clit. I scream in pain and frustration, but then my brain registers the vibration on my clit as pleasure again, not pain, and I remember the Master from my past could play this game all night. *Oh, dear god.*

* * * * *

Master pulls up a straight back chair and sits down. He motions for Pierre-Louis to kneel beside me. Folding his arms across his middle, he appears to be waiting. For what?

He commands Pierre-Louis, "You will observe her suffering."

Pierre-Louis lifts his chin and meets my gaze. For the first time I see that his eyes are swollen and red. He's been crying? *Oh hell.*

I watch the two men watching me. I wait for the *what next* but it doesn't seem forthcoming. Master says nothing. And I have nothing to say.

He said before I was still stubborn. What did that mean? Although, if I could see my own face, I'm sure my stubbornness would be reflected all over it.

Goddamn it. I did not return for this. "Peanut butter and jelly."

As soon as I say my safe words, I regret them. I don't know if it is the look of utter sadness and remorse on Master's face or the astonishment on Pierre-Louis'. Either way I don't have time to dwell on it. I am immediately released from my bonds and Master exits the room. He is followed closely by Pierre-Louis. What did I expect? Discussion? Debate? I know the house rules. When I feel it is time to safe-word, it is time to go. I made the choice. "Now I live with the consequences."

It is with a heavy heart that I climb the stairs from the dungeon. There isn't a soul in sight, not Master, or Pierre-Louis, or a single servant. I walk slowly through the great room, taking what I know is a final look around. "Goodbye dreams. Goodbye hope. Goodbye last chance at love."

I stagger, catching myself against the credenza. I stand sobbing, not able to take another step forward. What have I done? When did I become so weak?

"God, oh god," I beseech the ceiling, seeking answers that aren't there.

"Why did you return, Charlotte? Nostalgia?"

"I still love you. Desperately." *Crap. I said that out loud, didn't I?* "What I remembered of us — together — maybe I romanticized the best parts. Maybe I was forgetting the reality. Maybe I'm just not up to the reality of you anymore."

"So you forgot the pain?"

"No. I dreamed of the pain. I longed for it."

"Why?"

"Because I needed it."

"You could receive pain from anyone. There are a million websites that will direct you to someone more than willing to torture you."

"But they wouldn't cherish me as you once did."

He steps nearer. "I did cherish you. With my entire being. I never stopped."

"I can tell," I retort irritably.

"What does that mean?"

"I never stopped loving you. Even though you forced me away. Even though you refused to meet my needs."

"To give you children?"

"Yes!" I scream, tears sliding down my cheeks and snot spilling my nose. I breathe through my mouth between points. "I wanted a child. Did that make me a demon? You wouldn't even discuss it with me."

He steps closer, so close we are molded together in the front, so close we are breathing the same air. I am the one choking on snot and saliva. I've never felt so enraged, but then

I realize this anger has always been there. I hated him for not giving me a child.

"And any man's child would do?"

"I wanted yours."

"Any man's child would do," he repeats.

"Yes!" I seethe, spit flying out of my mouth.

His shoulders slump and years of sadness and heartbreak fill his eyes. "I couldn't give you a child, Charlotte."

My mouth drops open.

"I'm sterile. I have been since a childhood illness."

"God. Why didn't you tell me?"

"I was stupid. I thought you would leave me for my imperfection and I wanted you to stay because you loved me enough."

I left. I didn't love him enough. I close my eyes, knowing I would never change the decisions I made, even given a chance.

"It is a secret I've regretted not sharing with you in time to prevent you from leaving. I should have told you I was researching our fertility options but instead I left you in the dark…and then I awoke one day to find you'd gone."

I open my eyes and meet his gaze. "Why are you telling me this now?"

"Because I want there to never be a secret between us again. I don't want to lose you again."

"I safe-worded. I know the house rules. I have to leave." I attempt to pull away but he holds me in place.

"Maybe I have mellowed with age, but that is no longer a house rule."

No longer a house rule? My head spins with the implications. *I'm being given another chance?*

I meet his gaze. "I can stay?"

"The decision to stay or go is always yours. I would like very much for you to stay." He kisses me. "All I ask is no secrets, *oui*?"

It all becomes clearer. "I lust Pierre-Louis."

"That was obvious before you ever left for your holiday."

I nod and whisper, "I think I'm falling in love with him."

"*Oui*."

He seems very calm for a man I just told I love another. "I want to fall in love with you again."

"I too want nothing more."

Doubt fills my mind. I can't be the Cassiopeia I once was. I'm just not that tough anymore. "It's been a long time, Frankie. Are we asking for too much of each other? We obviously aren't the same people."

His lips descend on mine and his kiss prevents me from breathing at all but I don't pull away. I release all the emotion I've been holding in since I answered his summons…hell, since I left him twenty years ago. I choke on the mucus clogging my airway and he releases me. He tells me to "Blow".

There's no tissue, just his bare hand. I blow anyway. When I can breathe again, I explain, "I love the memory of who you were but I need to fall in love with the man you are now."

"And I need to learn to love the woman you are now, Charlotte. It has been a long time and you are no longer a young girl. I know I must change to accommodate who you have become, and honor your strengths and needs as they are now, not as they are remembered in my mind."

"It seems we have a lot of work to do."

"I'm willing to do my share."

"Me too."

He holds me and I hang on to him as if my life depends on not letting go.

"Tonight the three of us move into one bedroom, *oui*?"

I don't tell him of the jealousy-filled night I listened outside his bedroom door. I whisper, "I see no other way of making this work."

"Agreed and for proprietary sake, you will keep a bedroom for yourself in case you ever wish for your daughters to come for a visit."

"Thank you for understanding."

"I only wish they were mine."

The ache in his voice makes me know he's telling the truth. "We can't change the past, but we can share a future. I'm sorry I hurt you. I'm sorry I didn't trust you completely."

"As long as now you understand."

"I do."

* * * * *

Even though we are all in agreement to share a single bedroom, a single bed, when the moment comes I am as nervous and awkward as a virgin bride. I don't know what to expect. Will Pierre-Louis and Frankie make love to each other? Will the two men sandwich me? Will Master command the two of us, leaving us to obey?

I am standing in the adjoining bathroom, shaking and wringing my hands when Frankie knocks on the door. "Are you all right?"

"Yes?"

"Are you coming out soon?"

"Another minute?" My voice waivers.

The door opens a crack and he sees me standing in front of the mirror. "Can I come in?"

"Of course, Master."

He joins me in the large tiled room. "You are worried."

"It's obvious?"

He smiles, knowingly.

"I'm out of my element. I've never…I don't know what to do, or what to expect. I know, I know, you're the Master, I'm the slave. It's pretty easy. Just do what I'm told to do. No different than in the airplane. Or in the potting shed."

"It is different, though, isn't it?"

I release a breath I didn't realize I was holding. "It feels different."

"You have admitted you do not know me anymore, that you do not love me — "

"No. That isn't what I meant at all," I interrupt.

"Shh." He presses two fingers against my mouth. "Truth still the same. And you admitted you are already falling in love with Pierre-Louis."

Now I just feel horrible. It sounds so much worse when he says it. I run my hands over his shoulders. He still wears a crisp shirt and dress pants. Pierre-Louis and I have been nude since the dungeon. "I do love you. I just need to relearn *how* to love you."

"Americans always try to wrap the truth in a comforting lie to manage feelings. I am man enough to know I can earn your love again. You need not coddle me."

"Maybe I need to soften the truth a little for me," I say, sounding harsher than I intended.

"Perhaps." He makes a small face. "Because otherwise you couldn't have sex with me at all?"

"Not true."

"Then explain so I understand why you are hiding in the bathroom."

"You think I'm hiding from you? No, no, no."

"You are certainly not hiding from Pierre-Louis."

Reaching up, I cup his face. "I'm hiding from myself. I'm hiding from all that I'm feeling and all that I want to feel. I have doubts about *me*. Whether I will be able to relax and experience this for what it can be."

He takes my wrists in his but doesn't pull my hands from his face. His expression says he is trying to understand.

"Since returning to you, I have experienced amazing passion with Pierre-Louis but I've experienced no passion or tenderness from you. I'm afraid of how you will react once you see Pierre-Louis and me together. I worry Pierre-Louis and I will never be together sexually again. I worry you will want Pierre-Louis and not me. I worry I will never experience passion with you again."

He grabs my jaw, hurting a little, and kisses me, crushing my mouth, bruising my lips. I like his roughness and my mouth opens under the force of his kiss. My heart pounds inside my chest as I taste blood. John never kissed me like this. Pierre-Louis never kissed me like this...

His tongue pushes into my mouth, thrusting and stealing my breath. This I remember and it is even better than the nights I lay in fantasy, pretending I was still his.

He whispers into my mouth. "Am I still a good kisser, *mon amour*?"

"Better than I remembered."

He jerks my hair, pulling my head back and making my neck arch. His lips descend over my jugular, kissing, sucking, biting and making sensation arc through my body I have not felt in decades. "Oh god."

"Did you miss this a little?" His breath is warm and sweet on my cheek.

"A lot. I missed *this* a lot."

"Do you still doubt we will share passion again?"

"No. I know we will."

He lifts me on to the vanity and forces my legs apart as he jerks my hips forward, leaving me pressed hard against his hidden erection. "Are you most certain?"

"Most certain, Master. I feel the passion running through you."

"Who am I passionate for, Cassiopeia?"

"Me, Master. You are passionate for me."

His fingers find my folds and he opens me, thumbing my clit, finding my wetness. "Tell me you lust for me."

"I have always lusted for you, Master. I need you. I want you. Please, fuck me."

"Here? Now?"

"Yes, Master, yes. Please, yes." I grind invitingly against his fingers.

He calls to the other room, "Pierre-Louis, join us now." I cease functioning. I cease thinking. *Can I deal with this?*

The man in question appears immediately and I can't look at him. Master continues to thumb my clit, he bites my neck, and even though I am distracted by Pierre-Louis' mere presence I respond. I am embarrassed now that I am arching and moaning, whereas a moment ago I was completely immersed in feeling.

"Do you still want me to fuck you, Cassiopeia? Here? Now?"

I meet Master's gaze and am more unsure than I have ever been about anything but equally sure that I need to do this. Here. Now. Or risk losing everything. "Yes, Master."

He slides a finger into me slowly. "Is this what you want?"

"No, Master. Fuck me, please fuck me."

He holds my gaze as he continues sliding his finger in and out of me. I rock against his hand in response. "Why, Cassiopeia?"

"Because I lust you, Master."

"For now, that is enough. You will look at Pierre-Louis now."

What? Why? I don't ask. I shift my gaze and look at our shared lover. I expect to see hurt or anger, but all I see is lust. I lick my lips.

"Pierre-Louis, you will unfasten my trousers and pull them down for me."

He complies, and his gaze never leaves mine. Without looking I know the moment Master's cock is exposed. His tip rubs against my labia. I look back at Master. "Fill me, please, Master, don't make me wait."

His lips claim mine and I kiss him back with urgency and need. His length slides in, stretching me. I am still tender but I push the pain away and focus solely on the feeling of being filled by him. There are three of us in the room, but in that moment I am alone with my Master. I let him see the pain I have carried, the need. Our physical joining is no longer about lust or passion but reunion.

Chapter Twelve

ဢ

It is midday and I am lying by the pool, napping. I have been napping off and on since climbing out of bed this morning. It's been a week since Pierre-Louis and I returned from the bike tour, and my reunion with Master and the creation of the ménage has overshadowed all else, including sleep.

I am reminded I am not twenty-two anymore. *I am in love with two men.* And that's okay. Two men love me in return. It's a crazy thought and a reality I'm still adjusting to.

My eyes are hidden behind dark sunglasses. Between the sun glare from the water and the glinting light off the glass panes of the *orangerie*, I would be blind without them. Plus, it makes it easier to hide the fact that I have been sleeping, not reading the book in my lap. I think guiltily that it is Wednesday and if in Chicago, I would be up to my eyeballs in midweek research and paperwork. I sink deeper in my chaise, glad that I am here. I have to keep reminding myself that this is not a vacation, I do not have to be anxious that my time is running short...this is my life now...for as long as I desire it. I inhale sweet air, almost able to separate all the glorious scents that make it so—fresh-tilled soil, lavender, the blooms on the grapevines, the pine forest on the other side of the stables and of course the earthiness of the stables themselves. I smile, feeling the lull of sleep ease into my aching bones. The last few days seem like a dream. One I don't want to wake from.

"*Belle?*"

"Mmm?" I barely acknowledge Pierre-Louis' presence.

"Do not panic," he tells me, squatting beside me and covering my nakedness with an oversized towel. Of course I panic, sitting up, clutching the towel to my breasts.

"What has happened? What is wrong?" I gasp, pulling off my sunglasses to look at Pierre-Louis' concern-lined face, remembering that Frankie was going to the chai to check the progress of last year's barrels of wine. Every imaginable scenario goes through my mind, including he's hurt, he's dead. Oh god, please don't let him be dead.

"François asked me to inform you that your parents and daughters have just arrived and that they are waiting in the main salon. You are to please act surprised."

"Act surprised? How could I not act surprised. I'm naked, I'm wearing a collar...holy shit."

"I think you are panicking."

"Thank god you, at least, have clothes on."

He shrugs, "Just lucky. I went to the chai with François."

He went with Master? Was he invited? I wasn't invited. I pout, slightly disappointed, my entire forehead frowning as I wonder why he was invited to the winery and I wasn't...but then I remember my parents and children are waiting in the main salon to surprise me.

He blocks any view of the house as he helps me stand, suggesting, "The back stairs through the kitchen should get you to your room without anyone seeing you."

He shadows me as we walk, both of us knowing that if anyone looks through the main salon windows, they will probably see me...but at least I am wrapped in a towel.

"What are they doing here?" I ask out loud, knowing he has no more clue to that answer than I do. He stays with me, escorting me through the kitchen, up the back staircase, walks with me all the way to my room. And though it seems odd, I don't question his presence. I'm actually thankful he is near. I let out a deep sigh as I enter the bedroom, seeing the invisible servants have tidied, leaving no trace of the explosion in an insanity factory I left it. Now the room is as perfect as the first day I arrived, not a single thing out of place, my discarded clothing taken, presumably to the laundry. I blush, wondering about the toys, remembering that at least two vibrators, a butt plug, nipple clamps, actually two sets of nipple clamps, and assorted lubricants and massage oils had littered the nightstand when I left the room this morning.

Pierre-Louis helps me by pulling out several dresses and laying them across the bed.

"I'm supposed to be surprised to see my family. I think dressing for the occasion might be overdoing it."

He returns the dresses to the armoire. "What would you wear if you were sitting around on a Wednesday afternoon in Chicago?"

"Sweats and a t-shirt."

He looks despairingly through the armoire. "You didn't bring anything like that with you."

He turns toward the armoire and retrieves a pair of khaki capris and a pair of low-heeled leather sandals. "Put these on, I'll be right back."

I dress, wondering what top I can wear. Everything I brought with me is dressier than what I would ever wear at home. I am sitting in my bra and capris and buckling my sandal when he returns with a plain white t-shirt. He apologizes, "It might be a little loose, but it will be casual."

I pull it over my head. It isn't that loose, being a Lycra blend. I guess it would be skintight and very sexy on him. He ruffles my hair playfully and waggles his eyebrows.

"You look like a soccer mom."

I laugh. "I am a soccer mom, but thank you."

"For?" he asks.

"For being here, for helping me not be hysterical in this moment."

He kisses me gently before leading me from my room. With a heavy sigh, I head for the salon, preparing myself to act surprised when I see my daughters.

"Remember to act surprised," Pierre-Louis reminds me.

"Trust me, I'm still shell-shocked. Pretending surprise isn't going to be hard."

Seeing them, I throw my hands in the air and hoot. Though I needn't have tried so hard — after quick hugs, neither girl gave me a second glance, they were too busy drooling after Pierre-Louis. *Oh hell.*

We sit. A woman I've seen only once enters the room bearing a tray of refreshing drinks and small snacks. Frankie lifts a glass and toasts, "Welcome to France, welcome to my home."

My mother sits down on the couch beside me, sipping her drink. She whispers, "His age has settled well on him but then, I had no doubt. He was a very handsome young man, wasn't he?"

I smile tightly.

"And my, look at you," she says. "Coming to France has done wonders. It must be something in the water, you look ten years younger."

I try to look at my mother but am unsuccessful, I can't take my eyes off Pierre-Louis and the daughter standing on either side of him, keeping him cornered. His eyes are a little too wide, and I wonder if I should have warned him not to panic. I pay little attention to what my mother is saying but do look at her when she asks, "So are you sleeping with Frankie again?"

"Mother." I only realize after I have spoken my voice has become both loud and shrill as every eye turns toward me. I look at my father and smile even tighter, if that is possible, going to him to give him a hug. "You came to France. What a wonderful surprise. I can hardly believe you deviated from your planned attack of the Mediterranean. Was it twenty ports?"

"Twenty-three," he corrects. "And the trip isn't over. It's just with three women haranguing me to come here and make certain you are all right, I had little choice but to obey."

I laugh. "As you can see I'm well. I just needed a vacation and it seemed the perfect time to come to France when the invite was extended."

Bree pulls her besotted gaze from Pierre-Louis long enough to comment, "I didn't know you had friends in France. You should have told us."

I pat the cushion beside me, hoping to draw her away from the man, and am thankful when she joins me on the sofa. "François and I are old friends."

My mother interrupts, "Your mother did have a life before you were born...college, dating, lovers."

I turn my head and gape, bug-eyed. Beside me Bree giggles.

Ellie says from across the room, "I told her to find a boyfriend while we were away. I had no idea she would take me seriously."

Pierre-Louis chooses that moment to escape to the kitchen. "I will see how meal preparations are coming. You are staying for dinner, *oui*?"

"We don't want to be any trouble," my father says.

"No trouble," Pierre-Louis and Frankie say at the same time, causing their gazes to collide. Pierre-Louis turns a rosy shade of pink as he makes a quick exit.

"Will you be staying the night?" Frankie asks.

"No," my father insists, but he isn't heard over my mother and daughters' quick acceptance of his offer.

I let out a deep sigh. This should be entertaining.

But it isn't, it isn't entertaining at all as my mother's constant barbs go deeper and deeper. I'll be the first to admit that most of my adult life, we haven't had the best of relationships, but she's never been so completely confrontational before.

When Frankie drives everyone down to the stables to see his prized Andalusians, I finally escape out on to the terrace for some fresh air before dinner. I thought Mother had gone with them but when she suddenly joins me, I realize how wrong I was.

"Have I done something to you, Mother? Displeased you in some way?"

She shakes her head and comes nearer. "I don't want to see you hurt by this man again. Wasn't once enough?"

I rub at the tension in my forehead. "I left him, he didn't leave me."

"Of course you would say that now, but I was the one who had to watch your destruction. I had to see the light dim in your eyes until there was hardly anything left of you in their depths. Then finally, when you had the girls I had reason to hope you would heal and you rallied, but you were never the same...and now? We come here and I find your eyes are lit up with the excitement you once had...and yes, I'm angry that no one else could give you that much happiness. Not your father or I, not your beautiful daughters, not your husband."

My mouth opens and closes before I finally say, "It was nothing to do with any of you. I just never stopped loving him. It was hard being apart from him."

"And what happens when this ends? What happens when your vacation is over and you go back to Chicago? Are you going to make your children watch the light in your eyes die as I once did? Why would you do this to them?"

I gasp. "I'm not doing anything to them. The light in my eyes isn't going anywhere."

My mother clutches my hand, imploring, "Don't stay here. I beg you. Come with me and the girls."

"Madame?" Pierre-Louis calls from the open door.

"Yes, Pierre-Louis?"

"Could I beg your assistance in the kitchen one moment, please?"

"Of course." I walk away, leaving my mother on the terrace, telling myself that this doesn't have anything to do with the girls, but as I near the house I decide it has everything to do with my daughters...and I'm only trying to convince myself otherwise. I keep hearing my mother's final words as I left the terrace. *This isn't finished. We're going to talk about this. You're going to face the truth of a few things.*

I feel like a child again. A naughty, naughty child. And then I am face-to-face with my other lover.

In the sanctuary of the kitchen I bury my face in my hands and allow myself to be pulled into Pierre-Louis' chest by his strong arms. "God, thank you for the rescue."

"Is she always so intense?"

"Yes and no," I say. "It depends on what she's fighting for."

"What cause is she championing today?"

I shake my head. "I'm really not certain. I think *me.*"

"Perish the thought a mother might champion her daughter."

"She wants to rescue me from François."

Clanging pans make me jump and I realize suddenly that we are not alone in the kitchen. I step guiltily away from the embrace. I have gotten so used to the house having invisible staff and the three of us having the run of the place that I'd forgotten that Frankie actually does have employees. Pierre-Louis pulls me back into his arms. "You have nothing to hide from anyone here and I like holding you."

I look into his gaze and believe him...at least about the part where he likes holding me.

I am still not comfortable with strangers seeing me in Pierre-Louis' arms. I feel too old for him. Being with him makes me feel others will be as judgmental about this relationship as I once was with John and the younger women he snuck around with.

I feel like what we are sharing should be secret.

Oh god in merciful heaven, what am I doing trying to keep secrets from my mother, knowing she is like a hound on a scent trail? She will not let it go if she catches the scent of this…of us.

I want him to kiss me.

I want him to hold me in his insanely beautifully muscled arms and tell me I am beautiful and sexy, even though he told me those exact words only a few hours ago. I know my suddenly deflated confidence is because the green-eyed monster of jealousy was seriously freaked out my daughters were looking at him as if they could gobble him up. It wasn't worries they might discover our secret, I was feeling possessive. Pierre-Louis is mine.

Oh hell.

I take his hand and drag him into the walk-in pantry, closing the door behind us. His eyebrow hikes with concern. "Do you want to tell me to stay away from the dining room tonight?"

"No," I shake my head. "I want you there. I want you on my left and Frankie on my right as we sit every night. I want your undivided attention. I want you to laugh at my jokes and I want you to entertain me with your stories. I don't want to feel like I am competing with anyone else."

"There is no other for me. I am François' and I am yours."

"My daughters—"

"Are little girls who do not interest me. Is that what you fear? That I will compare you to their youth?"

I nod.

"If anything, I will compare them, but I will be thinking what beautiful women they are to become as they grow up, more and more resembling you."

"How is it a Frenchman always knows exactly what to say?"

He smiles, bending his head to kiss me soundly. "Relax. Everything will be fine."

As we leave the pantry, I hope dinner goes as well as he promises, but as the night progresses I know there isn't a chance in hell it will.

My daughters are very vivacious, persuasive young women, well skilled in the art of dinner conversation, barely letting anyone else say anything at all, except each other, and both ladling compliment upon praise directed at Pierre-Louis. He laughs at their jokes, he panders to their vanity. He is a typical man surrounded by beautiful women and soaking in their adoration.

I kick him beneath the table, hoping it bruises.

By the time dinner is over and everyone has retired to their bedrooms, my nerves are shot and I want nothing but to be left alone.

The greenhouse seems the perfect place to escape to. The damp heat of the day collected and condensed in the greenhouse is a small comfort. The scent of earth and exotic flora permeates my senses, soothing my soul...until Pierre-Louis walks in.

"You flirted with my daughters," I accuse, knowing he did no such thing and if anything was the perfect gentleman, deflecting the compliments back to them...which to a teen girl I knew would seem like flirting...

He defends, "I didn't."

"I know you tried not to, but they are both still hot for you."

"That I did not encourage." He bristles, bellowing like a true Frenchman can.

"I know," I shout back, shouting only because he is…and because I am so frustrated. I bury my face in my hands. "They are infatuated with you."

"*Oui,*" he admits to noticing.

I shake my head. "I can't do this."

"Do what?"

"This. Us." I gesture frantically between us. "Keep having sex with you."

"Sex?" he huffs.

"Yes, sex, knowing both of my daughters want to have sex with you too. It makes me feel—perverted."

He turns away hurt, pouting.

I frown, not meaning to make him feel bad but unable to change the way I feel. I beg, "Do not pull the pouting Frenchman act on me."

"This is not an act. For you, maybe, because for you, it was just sex, but for me? We are beginning a relationship. I thought what we were sharing meant something to you as well." He storms from the *orangerie* and Frankie walks in through the door before it slams closed, announcing, "That went well."

"Don't start on me. I didn't ask for this, I didn't ask for any of this."

"No?"

"No," I say, pacing. The fronds of a palm tickle my cheek as I pass and I brush it away angrily. I insist, "I was happy. My life was fine before you showed back up."

"Was it, really?" he asks sarcastically, keeping his distance. Smart man. I want to punch something, a wall perhaps, but the walls here are all glass and the thought of stitches doesn't appeal. Hitting him, on the other hand, might make me feel much better.

I admit, "No. It wasn't and you know it wasn't. You talked with Paulette, I'm sure she told you everything, how miserable I was, how lonely."

"She only told me you had grown old. Resigned to the life you were living. She believed your spirit was dying."

I march up to him and poke him in his chest, "And you thought you would arrive like a knight in shining armor and rescue me? Doesn't that make me sound pathetic? Yes, my life was different, I was trying to survive a bout of empty-nest depression, but I would have figured it out."

"*Oui*, you would have, I never said that you were not a strong woman. You didn't need me but I wanted you, and that makes me selfish. Perhaps I should have left you alone."

I watch as Frankie turns and starts to walk away from me. I let out a sob I wasn't aware I was holding. "No, you shouldn't have. I've missed you and I've loved being back...this just won't work. There is no way to make this work."

"Honesty would make it work."

"You want me to tell my daughters the truth about our relationship?"

"Perhaps not all of the details, but the important ones, how you feel about me, how you feel about Pierre-Louis."

"I can't do that."

"Why not?" He shrugs nonchalantly as only Frenchmen can do when they are demanding the impossible. "Are you afraid you will offend their fine moral upbringing?"

"Do not make fun of my life."

"On the contrary, I commend you. Your children are amazing, intelligent women. On the other hand, do you believe them fools that they cannot see that you are in love with both of us?"

"Love?" I snort, thinking how ridiculous this moment is. "I cannot tell my daughters I am in love with two men."

From behind me, Pierre-Louis whispers, "Is it true you do?"

I jump and turn toward him. I hadn't realized he'd come back into the greenhouse. He stalks toward me, grabbing my face between his palms before pulling me toward him, our lips colliding. Frankie is there immediately, behind me, molded to my back as Pierre-Louis is molded to my front. He kisses the back of my neck, alternating painful nibbles with teasingly soft kisses. This isn't fair. Really it isn't. Especially when they trade, pivoting me between them so that Frankie is suddenly kissing my mouth and Pierre-Louis is dropping kisses over the back of my neck.

Lightning goes up and down my spine, need speeds through my veins. It doesn't matter how often they hold me between them like this. I do not think I will ever get used to the increased sensation of both of them at the same time.

Frankie pulls away, leaving me gasping, dizzy around the edges. "You didn't answer the question," he whispers, catching and holding my gaze, demanding honesty. I don't look away.

"Yes, I am falling back in love with you. I was insane to believe I had fallen out of love with you. And I am falling in love with Pierre-Louis, but you already knew that."

"He did not know." He nods toward Pierre-Louis and I realize I haven't come close to saying anything remotely like that to him.

I turn to face Pierre-Louis when I feel the pressure of his hands on my waist to do so. Our gazes lock and I can see the emotion filling his eyes. His voice is thick when he demands, "Tell me."

I smile and release the breath I've been holding. "I love you, Pierre-Louis. *Je t'aime.*"

Frankie turns me to face him. Tears glisten in his eyes. "I could have asked for nothing more. Nothing less."

I caress his cheek. "I love you, François Rene de Hart."

He kisses my hand. "I know."

We end up in a sandwich hug, me between two men and I couldn't be happier, but our quiet moment is ripped apart by Bree and Ellie shrieking at each other. The last time I saw them they were both going into their bedrooms, so I can't imagine what happened between then and now. With them, I can only imagine. I hurry outside to silence the commotion if not resolve their differences.

Finding them poolside, I demand, "What is going on? You aren't at home. You are guests here. You don't act this way." I realize they are dressed to go out, both of them wearing beaded, spaghetti-strap dresses. I point at chairs. "Sit down."

They are silent and sulky but at least they obey.

I sit too, shaking, hating that I just sounded like a mother of toddlers instead of grown women. Looking at them both, I demand, "Now just what is going on? And where in the hell do you think you are going this time of night?"

"We came out here to find Pierre-Louis because we want to go clubbing but then we got in a fight about which one of us has dibs." They look at each other accusingly, then their expressions twist. It is like watching a mirror as their faces go soft around the edges. I think I know what this is about but don't really want to acknowledge the possibility. I turn my head to look behind me, seeing Pierre-Louis. He is wearing his swimming trunks and, muscles stretching, he dives. Great. A moonlit swim. Now?

"Dibs?" I gasp, then laugh almost hysterically. "Are you serious?"

"I wanted him first."

"I'm oldest."

"You already had a fling with the writer."

I stand, irritated. "Enough. Neither one of you can have him."

"Mom," Bree whines, "he isn't too old."

"No," I agree, pacing beside the pool. My eyes are drawn to Pierre-Louis' powerful strokes. I see Frankie has joined us poolside and is sitting with his pants rolled up and feet dangling in the pool. When did my life become a sideshow? I pace back to face my girls, admitting, "And he isn't too young."

I pull a chair closer and sit between them. "There's something you need to know."

They look at me with wide eyes, waiting. It takes me a moment to build up my courage, even though I had all night to worry about it and run possible scenarios and conversations through my head. I decide they are adults now, and I might as well treat them like they are, but it seemed so much easier when it was just an idea in my head. A brave plan. I finally admit, "We're lovers. Since you are both obviously old enough to be fighting over which one of you gets to have sex with him, you are old enough to know I have already claimed him as my own."

Their jaws drop and then they look from me to him.

Ellie responds first. "Shit."

Bree stays silent and I can't tell if she is merely sullen, too shocked for words, or angry. She recovers enough to say, "Grandma said you were lovers with François. That you dated a long time ago."

I let out a deep sigh. "Well, your grandmother had no business saying anything at all, but since she did, yes, we were."

I do not want to go any further with this conversation. I cannot believe I just admitted what I did. Something about seeing them both look at Pierre-Louis with such obvious lust. "This really wasn't supposed to come up in conversation. You're only here another day."

If I thought to shift their focus I was wrong.

"Isn't François mad? I mean, isn't he still interested?" Ellie demands.

I look away, embarrassed, and watch Pierre-Louis swim. His muscles bulge, glistening with water. God, he's beautiful. Can I blame my daughters? He swims over to the pool edge and hangs from the side, talking softly with Frankie. Catching them both looking at me, I blush and look down at my hands in my lap.

"He still loves you," Bree accuses. "Don't you even care that you are going to break his heart if he finds out about Pierre-Louis? Didn't having Daddy cheat on you teach you how horribly affairs end?"

They both sit looking at me, one curious, one horrified.

"You are too young for this conversation. Damn it, girls. I'm too young for this conversation."

"He knows?" Ellie guesses.

I nod. "We have an arrangement—the three of us."

"Oh my god, you're talking about a ménage," Bree gasps. "I may puke."

"That is so French," Ellie says. "Wait until I tell my friends."

"What? No." I gasp. "What happens in this family—"

"Mom, really. You are the coolest mom on the planet," Ellie declares, standing and kissing me on top of the head. She turns to Bree. "You owe me twenty bucks."

Bree stands. I can't read her expression and that bothers me. She shrugs at Ellie and asks, "Still want to go clubbing?"

"No, wait," I say, catching Bree's hand. "I don't want you to be mad at me, or hate me."

She screws up her face. "Why would you think that?"

"You're disgusted enough by what I told you that you want to puke."

She rolls her eyes. "Thinking about you having sex with either of them would make me want to puke. I mean...really...you're my mother. I don't want to think about that. I just didn't want Ellie to be right."

"Right?" I ask, still confused.

"About Pierre-Louis. She said you had to be sleeping with him. He couldn't take his eyes off of you all night and you were positively drooling through dinner, but I didn't want to see that."

I hug her close, tears falling over my cheeks. "So we're okay?"

She hugs me back. "Yes. I love you, Mom."

They walk away, huddled close, whispering and giggling. I think I can officially have a nervous breakdown now. Pierre-Louis lifts himself out of the pool in a smooth move and pads over to me. He drips as he kneels. "Everything okay?"

"No. I don't think everything will ever be okay again. I just admitted to my daughters that I'm in a ménage with two men."

"*Oui*, a ménage is three. It makes sense there are two men."

I smack his wet shoulder. "I'm humiliated. What was I thinking?"

"You were thinking honesty is the best policy. It keeps things from getting messy. Not that I would have, but they were obviously interested." He shrugs and the mannerism is so male, so French, the nonchalance. "Relax. The cat is out of the bag now. You can loosen up now. You can be yourself again."

Frankie joins us, sitting in the chair Ellie vacated. "So, all is well again?"

"They took the news remarkably well." I lean forward to press a kiss to his cheek and have the worst thought. "Oh shit. My parents. They wouldn't tell my parents, right?"

Frankie shrugs.

"That isn't helpful," I tell him tersely as I race after my girls to tell them the information I shared was completely

166

confidential. His laughter follows me and I shout back to him, "I'm glad I'm entertaining someone."

"Entertaining? Is that what you call it?"

Mortified, I stand and face my mother. One look at her face and I know the girls have already told her *everything*.

"I don't believe this. What did Ells and Bree do, race straight up to your room with their discovery?"

Mother shrugs. "Ellie texted both me and your father."

"A text?" I repeat, appalled, not believing she would reveal my darkest secrets in a text. "And probably a hundred of her closest friends," I say sarcastically, noting the two men in my life have simultaneously disappeared while my back was turned. *Cowards.*

"She's *your* daughter." She walks over to the edge of the pool and sits, dangling her feet.

"Yes, she is." I grin a little. *The little girl most like me.* Geesh. I slip off my shoes and join my mother. The water seems as warm as bath water. It would almost be relaxing…if.

She speaks in hushed tones, as if we're sharing secrets. "I can't believe you told them. A ménage. Really. What are you thinking? At your age?"

"Age didn't stop you from buying a French maid costume, or sharing the fact you did with my daughters."

"Touché. Still, sweetheart, are you sure about this?"

"Can anyone ever be sure in matters of the heart?"

"Yes," she states matter-of-factly. "I knew the instant I laid eyes on your father I would marry him. It was love at first sight."

I bump my shoulder against hers. "I guess I'm like you in that aspect then. I knew the moment I saw Frankie my heart would be his forever. Though I think with Pierre-Louis lust came before love."

"With Pierre-Louis lust would be the first reaction for any woman," my mother titters.

I can't hold back my own chortle. "He is gorgeous."

My mother sighs. "That's an understatement…but do you love him?"

"I do. It's a young love, in its infancy, but love still the same."

"I pity you, loving two men. Your father drives me insane enough thank you very much."

"I must say, Mom, you're taking this better than I expected."

"What? You think I've gotten to this age without seeing a few things? All that matters to me is that your eyes are twinkling again…and you seem genuinely happy."

"I am."

"Well then, you'll understand that we're getting back on the road in the morning."

"So soon? You just got here," I exclaim, alarmed that Dad isn't taking this news as well as my mother and daughters.

"We forced your father from his itinerary. Now that he knows you are not only alive and well, but happy, he's ready to get back to the previously scheduled vacation."

"So, he's okay with my being here."

"You mean, with both of them?"

I shrug. She never did pull her punches.

"It'll take some getting used to, but honestly he just wants you happy. All we've ever wanted was for you to be happy." She admits, "I've always hated John. He had twitchy eyes and a dishonest mouth."

Now she tells me this. "You could have mentioned it before the wedding."

"We assumed you were already pregnant with the Frenchman's brat, and when he wouldn't marry you, you took the first sucker you could rope in."

"Mother."

She shrugs. "What else could we think? You sat around crying for months and then you're suddenly getting married?"

I sigh. In hindsight, the circumstances were suspect. "That couldn't have been further from the truth. And the girls are John's."

"That's obvious *now*. They look just like him."

I grimace, preferring to believe they look absolutely nothing like John.

"You do know the new problems this presents?"

"*New* problems?" I have no idea what she's talking about.

"Well, we can't keep the girls on vacation forever. Sooner or later they will have to return home. Will they return to an empty house or will you be there waiting for them?"

I start counting weeks until fall semester. I know they are planning on attending.

.

Chapter Thirteen

☙

"Alone at last."

Smiling, I turn and face Frankie. I go to him, happy when he sweeps me into his arms and holds me tight. "I was afraid you weren't going to survive that."

"Master?"

"Your parents? Your daughters? I thought you might come to your senses and leave with them."

"I came to my senses when I answered your summons."

He smiles down into my face. "You mean that, don't you?"

"Yes. I've missed you terribly over the years. I can't tell you how often I've driven by the manse, hoping for a glimpse of you."

"I didn't know."

I sigh, feeling sad. "We've lost so much time together."

He hugs me tighter. "We're together now."

I smile, but it is tight. I'm still feeling shaky with my new reality of being loved by two men. Especially having been faced with the youth and vitality of my daughters. I can't help but fear that our future may not be as happy as the present. What happens when Pierre-Louis grows tired of both of us because of our age? I don't dare voice my fears. I rest my head against Frankie's shoulder.

"Are you going to tell me what's on your mind?"

I shake my head.

"Am I going to have to beat it out of you?"

I gasp, knowing there is no idleness in the threat. I meet his gaze, admitting, "New day, same worries."

"Ahh." He kisses my forehead. "You don't think I've had the same insecurities? I love him and I believe him when he says he loves me. All we can do is have faith our love is strong enough to withstand the difficulties."

"And old age?" I ask.

"*Oui.* And old age."

He kisses me gently. "No matter what we'll have each other from now on."

"Yes," I agree without reservation.

He smacks my bottom suddenly and it stings deep. "You are still wearing clothes. You don't remember what happened last time you broke the house rule?"

I smile into his chest before stepping back a little to meet his gaze. I could argue my parents and daughters only just pulled out of the driveway, but I don't. Without comment, I pull my top over my head and drop it to the ground at his feet. I remove my bra, pants, and panties with quick motions, dropping each garment similarly. "Burn them all. I like being naked with you."

"Don't tempt me." He takes a long appreciative look at me.

I smile, feeling voluptuous and sexy. I'm not a child anymore, and I've learned a little over the years about using my feminine wiles. I lick my lips and, backing away, hold out my hand to him.

He catches my hand and lets me pull him toward the stairs. "What's this?"

"Want me a little?" I tease, backing up the stairs.

"A little? A lot." Frankie follows.

I smile a little wider before catching my bottom lip between my teeth. "That's good. Very good. Because I'm still making up for two decades of neglect."

"Neglect, was it? I seem to remember some procreating in the midst of all that *neglect*."

"John was not an adept lover."

"*Non?*"

"No."

"So while we were apart what did you crave most? The pleasure? The pain?"

"I have to choose?" I pout, stumbling on a step.

Frankie catches me and lifts me into his arms. "Call me curious. Did you fantasize about me?"

"Every night." I wrap my arms around his neck as he strides purposely toward our room. He keeps walking, going to the next room, the one originally designated as mine. Whether intentional or unintentional, Frankie makes me think about Pierre-Louis and I wonder where he is, what he is doing. I haven't seen him since before I said goodbye to my parents and the girls.

"And? Did you think about my kisses? My cane?" He pushes open the door with his foot.

"Both. I never separated one from the other."

He drops me on the bed, steps out of his shoes and starts to disrobe. "What about now?"

"Now?" I'm confused.

He drops his shirt on to a side chair's cushioned seat. He follows suit with his slacks and underwear. He stands before me. Naked. Strong. Charismatic. How did I ever leave him? It boggles my mind that my desire for children was *that* strong.

I hold out my hand to him, wanting to pull him into the bed.

He shakes his head.

"I like having you as a lover," I admit. "I like that this time around our relationship is more playful and less..." I try to think of the right word. *Militant* comes to mind but that is too strong. *Strict* seems both right and wrong. "Structured."

He seems to mull that over for a moment then takes my hand. "I like being your lover, Cassiopeia. But there's still room for play, *for discipline.*"

I shiver, feeling the edge of a threat. *I haven't done anything I deserve to be punished for.* He covers my body with his.

"I like feeling you tremble. It excites me knowing that you fear me."

He pushes up on to his hands and meets my gaze.

I accuse, "Sadist."

"Guilty," he admits, smiling broadly. "I never claimed otherwise."

I love his smile. He does that a lot more now than then. I wonder if it is because he has mellowed with age, or if Pierre-Louis wrought this miraculous change in his personality. I can't imagine being in Pierre-Louis' company for very long without smiling and laughing. He seems to bring out that part in most people. I wonder again where he is, and again push the thought away.

I am happy and content when Frankie pushes his hard length inside me. "God, Frankie. I missed your cock."

He chuckles. I know that he's very aware of how well-endowed he is.

"I'm not as long or as thick as Pierre-Louis."

I think about that for a moment. I'd have never considered either. "I disagree, Master."

"I am not as vain as I once was. I can look at the truth in things and not feel threatened."

If that is true then he certainly has matured beyond any hope I'd ever held to. "I'm not trying to flatter you. It is the truth as I see it. You are both very nicely endowed. Equally so. And you have more experience to know exactly what to do with your length and girth."

He bellows.

"I'm telling you the truth. I don't have to tell you to 'fuck me like you mean it' because you always do."

He looks serious when he asks, "Is this true?"

I nod.

"Then my young Pierre-Louis has definitely been holding back."

He kisses me before I can say anything else, thrusting deeper as he does so. I grunt with the force, stretching to take the rest of him deeper. I know the instant he sinks completely in. I am filled as deeply as I can ever be filled. The sensation pulls at emotion deep in my chest and, as he sets up a deep rhythm, tears fill my eyes.

"This I've missed most, Frankie. *This.* No one has ever loved me, cherished me as you do."

He kisses away my tears. "*Vous êtes mon coeur et âme, mon amour. Vous êtes la moitié qui me rend tout entier.*"

You are my heart and soul, my love. You are the half that makes me whole. "Yes. You always said that perfectly. I always believed you meant every word because I feel the same way."

"Don't leave me again, Charlotte."

"Not a chance, Frankie. We've been given a second time around. I won't blow it again."

"You did not, as you say, blow it. You did what you needed to do. You do not regret your daughters and I do not ever want you to. It is as I needed to do when I sent you the bustier. I could not live with myself another minute if I did not pursue you again." He kisses me and I cling to him, cling to his words as he whispers again and again, "*Je t'aime, Je t'aime.*"

* * * * *

The sun is sinking when I roll over to face him, finally brave enough to ask, "Where is Pierre-Louis?" without fear of ruining the moment.

I lay in his arms and he squeezes me closer. "I sent him on an errand that will take him a few days to complete."

"Oh really?"

He smiles suspiciously. "For the winery. Either I had to go or he had to go, and I decided he has had more than enough alone time with you. It is my turn to have you all to myself. He was much put out."

I snicker.

His eyes twinkle and I suddenly understand just what my mother was saying. Happiness. Mischievousness. Passion for life. I see it all and more in his eyes. I settle against him, feeling content. "I'm glad you chose to stay here with me."

"There was no more choice than to take my next breath. I must be here with you. We have been too long apart."

Ah, Frenchmen. They do have a way of making a girl feel special.

Also by Roxy Harte

ঝ

eBooks:

Chronicles of Surrender 1: Sacred Secrets
Chronicles of Surrender 2: Sacred Revelations
Chronicles of Surrender 3: Unholy Promises
Chronicles of Surrender 4: Echo of Redemption
Chronicles of Surrender 5: Cries of Penance
Debonair Dyke
Prodigal Slave

About Roxy Harte

Multi-published author Roxy Harte has loved erotic romance novels since she stumbled across her first at the tender age of thirteen. Since she especially loves books that offer strong insight into the characters' psyches, as a writer she wants to provide readers with characters who are not only charismatic and engaging, but also intellectually, spiritually and sexually complex. When she started writing in earnest twelve years ago, it provided an evening respite from the full-time care of her invalid mother and Alzheimer-diagnosed father, and although both of her parents died a decade ago, she now writes so that her readers may find a small escape of their own at the end of a tedious day.

Roxy lives in southwestern Ohio in a small town bordered by fields and railroad tracks, with her husband and collegiate daughter, two boisterous dogs, Petey and Jazzi, and five cats, Miss Kitty, Sadie, Dharma, Karma and Tilak.

The author welcomes comments from readers. You can find her website and email address on her author bio page at www.ellorascave.com.

Tell Us What You Think

We appreciate hearing reader opinions about our books. You can email us at Service@ellorascave.com (when contacting Customer Service, be sure to state the book title and author).

Why an electronic book?

We live in the Information Age—an exciting time in the history of human civilization, in which technology rules supreme and continues to progress in leaps and bounds every minute of every day. For a multitude of reasons, more and more avid literary fans are opting to purchase e-books instead of paper books. The question from those not yet initiated into the world of electronic reading is simply: *Why?*

1. *Price.* An electronic title at Ellora's Cave Publishing runs anywhere from 40% to 75% less than the cover price of the exact same title in paperback format. Why? Basic mathematics and cost. It is less expensive to publish an e-book (no paper and printing, no warehousing and shipping) than it is to publish a paperback, so the savings are passed along to the consumer.

2. *Space.* Running out of room in your house for your books? That is one worry you will never have with electronic books. For a low one-time cost, you can purchase a handheld device specifically designed for e-reading. Many e-readers have large, convenient screens for viewing. Better yet, hundreds of titles can be stored within your new library—on a single microchip. There are a variety of e-readers from different manufacturers. You can also read e-books on your PC or laptop computer. (Please note that Ellora's Cave does not endorse any specific brands.

You can check our website at www.ellorascave.com for information we make available to new consumers.)

3. *Mobility.* Because your new e-library consists of only a microchip within a small, easily transportable e-reader, your entire cache of books can be taken with you wherever you go.

4. *Personal Viewing Preferences.* Are the words you are currently reading too small? Too large? Too… ANNOYING? Paperback books cannot be modified according to personal preferences, but e-books can.

5. *Instant Gratification.* Is it the middle of the night and all the bookstores near you are closed? Are you tired of waiting days, sometimes weeks, for bookstores to ship the novels you bought? Ellora's Cave Publishing sells instantaneous downloads twenty-four hours a day, seven days a week, every day of the year. Our webstore is never closed. Our e-book delivery system is 100% automated, meaning your order is filled as soon as you pay for it.

Those are a few of the top reasons why electronic books are replacing paperbacks for many avid readers.

As always, Ellora's Cave welcomes your questions and comments. We invite you to email us at Service@ellorascave.com or write to us directly at Ellora's Cave Publishing Inc., 1056 Home Avenue, Akron, OH 44310-3502.

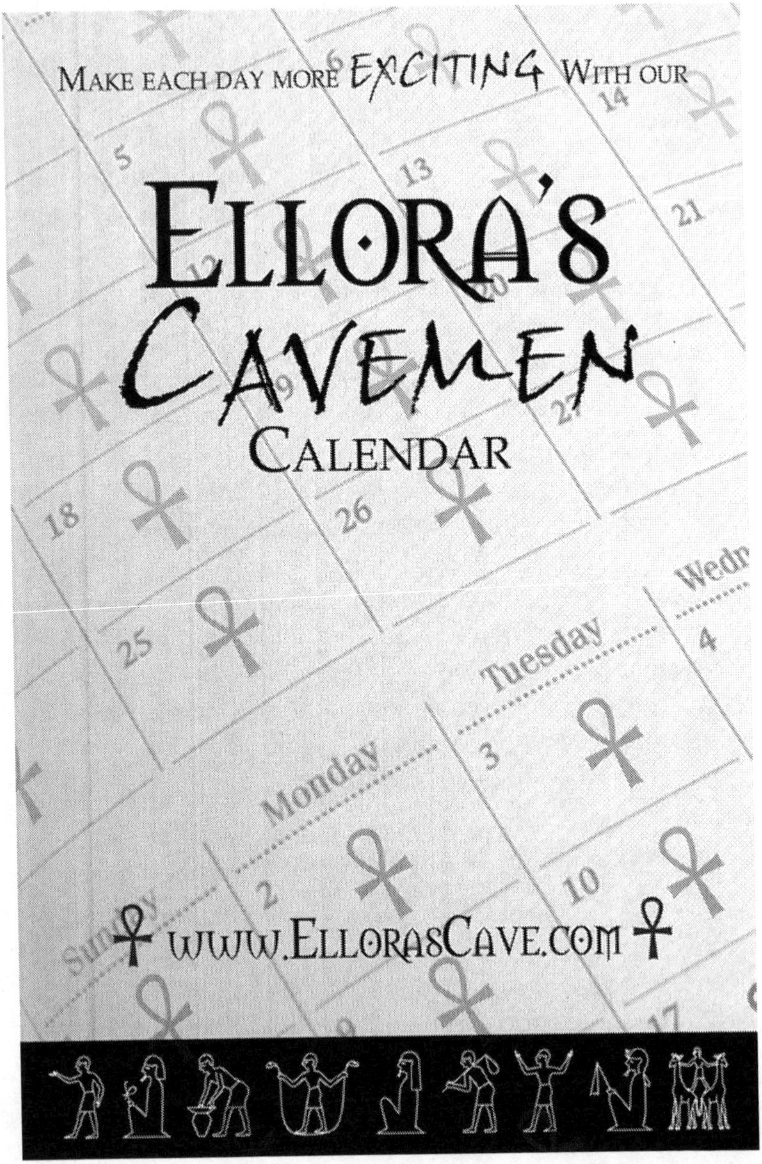
Make each day more EXCITING with our
Ellora's
Cavemen
Calendar
www.EllorasCave.com

ELLORA'S CAVE
Romanticon

Annual convention
for women who
refuse to behave

www.ECRomanticon.com
For additional info contact: conventions@ellorascave.com

Made in the USA
San Bernardino, CA
16 September 2015